The High Pasture

YOUNG AMERICA BOOK CLUB
A Division of Weekly Reader Children's Book Club

Presents

The High Pasture

RUTH HARNDEN

Illustrated By Vee Guthrie

Houghton Mifflin Company Boston

The Riverside Press Cambridge

1 9 6 4

To MONICA and BILL

1

THE steep mountain trail widened abruptly to an open view of the valley below, and Tim McCloud, half running down the slope, skidded to a stop on the slippery pine needles that carpeted the path. From here he could look down on the roofs of the sprawling ranch, the big rambling house, the wide barns and smaller sheds. In the high, clear air distances were deceptive. Everything looked to be closer at hand than it really was. Now, for example, it seemed as though he could make a broad jump from right here and land on the roof of the ranch house. He wished he could. He wanted to tell Aunt Kate what he had seen in the high pasture. If the roof was anywhere near as close as it looked he'd try the jump. But he'd been here barely two weeks and he'd already learned that a mountain that looked ten minutes away could be a whole day's journey on horseback. The ranch was actually more than half a mile below him, and even running and sliding it would take him some time to reach it. He contented himself with looking while he caught his breath from the fast descent.

It was a pleasant sight, the sunlit green meadows, sprinkled with wildflowers, that flared widely at either side of the cluster of old buildings. The original house was of unpeeled logs. The barns and sheds were slab-sided. But all of them had weathered by now to a uniform gingerbread brown, and had taken on a soft, blurred look as if they might in fact be made of gingerbread. No one could call them pretty. They simply looked comfortable, and as if they belonged to the land.

For the first time since he'd come here Tim realized that he was looking at it all almost as if he belonged, almost as if he were coming home. For days he had only felt strange, and homesick, and like someone exiled from all he loved. Well, actually he had got through the days very well. There was so much to keep him busy, and everything was so new to him that he'd got interested in spite of himself. But the nights were lonely, and haunted by bad dreams. He dreamed about his mother, and all the fears he didn't face by day would come out in his dreams. He waked up shaking with fright, and once or twice he had waked up crying. He told himself that dreams were unfair, sneaking up on you when you were helpless and giving you no choice. They were like something going on behind your back. They were a mean trick. And then he wondered if the dreams were a warning? But he never let himself think about that for very long. He'd get up fast, and then dig out his mother's last letter and reread it before he even got dressed. That always made him feel better.

The pleasure he was feeling right now was touched with pride, and with a sort of protective feeling that was wholly new to him. Maybe that was because of the scare he'd had on the mountain? But why should he feel any pride? Well, he'd heard about the ranch all his life, and about Aunt Kate who had homesteaded it. Actually Aunt Kate was his father's aunt, and Tim's great-aunt. What a strange sort of woman, he used to think as he listened to the stories his father told. What an odd thing for a young woman — little more than a girl at the time — to leave the city and go out and homestead like a man. First she'd taken a quarter section, a hundred and sixty acres. By now, many years later, she had a whole section of six hundred and forty acres. She had done it all herself, raising cattle, dealing with horse thieves, even mending her own roads. Tim had imagined her as a giant of a woman, and he was prepared to be afraid of her. When she'd met him at the bus terminal, two weeks ago, she had had to introduce herself, and even then he could hardly believe that this was Aunt Kate.

"I guess you're Tim," she had said, looking up into his face. Tim was thirteen and a little tall for his age, but he certainly hadn't expected to be taller than Aunt Kate. She was one of the smallest women he'd ever seen, and just at first he thought she must be one of the oldest. But there was one thing he had no doubt about — he'd never in his life seen anyone so oddly dressed. She wore faded whipcord riding breeches, leather puttees and boy's moccasins. But over her head and shoulders, and falling to her waist, she wore a lacy lavender shawl. From the folds of the shawl her delicate, worn face looked out with the eyes of a bright bird.

"You look like your father," she said, "and I guess you're going to be as big, to judge from the size of your feet." At once Tim shifted his feet uncomfortably. Did she notice everything? And didn't she ever smile? His mother had about the nicest smile in the world, and she smiled a lot. Well, he'd expected to be afraid of Aunt Kate, and he was. At the same time he wondered how anyone could be afraid of such a very tiny and such a very old lady.

4

But there was something about Aunt Kate that didn't seem old, and there was something about her that seemed terribly strong.

"Follow me," she said then, and she turned abruptly and strode off. He had to move quickly to keep up with her. She walked with the quick, springing step of a boy. From the back you might almost take her for a boy — if it wasn't for that crazy shawl! In the next minute Tim realized why she wore the shawl. She had a hump on her back. Now it came to him that his father had told him about this. It just didn't seem to go with anything else he'd ever heard about her, and so he'd forgotten it until now.

He followed her out of the bus terminal, and around the corner of the building into a narrow side street. "Put your bags in the back," she said as she herself leapt nimbly onto the driving seat of a sort of cart or buggy that was hitched to two horses and standing by the curb. Tim had expected a car, however old and queer, but his surprise was lost in admiration of the horses. They were as red as Irish setters and their coats gleamed as if they'd been polished. When he'd put his two bags onto the small platform behind the seat, he climbed up, a little awkwardly, to the seat beside Aunt Kate.

"What are their names?" he asked her, still admiring the horses. "Dexter and Sinister," she said. After a second she added, "Get it?" and turned to glance at him briefly with her bright, unsmiling eyes. "Uh — oh!" he said, "right and left." It was sort of funny. At least he guessed it was a kind of joke, though Aunt Kate still didn't so much as smile. "Raised 'em from colts," she told him. "Broke 'em and trained 'em myself. And if I do say so, there's no finer matched pair in the county."

"Do they always just stand like that, without being tied?" he asked. They didn't look docile; they looked proud and spirited. "Always have," she said. "That's what I mean by training, though some people think they've done it if they can get 'em between shafts and keep a bit in their mouths." She'd lifted the reins as she talked and at once the horses set off at a smart trot. " 'Course," she added fairly, "I wouldn't swear to what they might do in the city. If they ever saw a motorcycle I'd likely never see them again."

Tim had never before ridden in anything drawn by horses and he was fascinated by the motion, and by the sense of speed. Funny, but it seemed faster than riding in a car. It was partly, perhaps, his exposed position. The carriage had no roof or hood of any kind so that he was sitting right out in the air, and the air seemed to be rushing past him. It had the excitement of a slight danger, and it made him feel a little the way he felt when he was sledding a fast slope.

"What do you call this — er — wagon?" he asked her.

"You don't call it a wagon," she told him crisply. "It's a buckboard." For a second she turned and looked at him. "You've got a lot to learn," she said. Tim nodded. "That's what Dad said. He said I'd learn a lot." For a minute he felt as if a cloud had passed over him. It was almost as tangible as an actual cloud that might have passed over the sun to chill him. He shivered slightly, thinking about his father, remembering all the reasons for his being here.

"How was your mother when you left?" Aunt Kate broke into his thoughts to ask. He didn't want to think about that. He certainly didn't want to talk about it to this strange woman who spoke in such a spare and cold sort of way. He had to force himself to answer. "I guess she's pretty sick," he said in a fast, nervous voice that grated on his own ears. He cleared his throat and tried to do better. "Dad says she may be in the hospital most of the summer, and that's why — " he stopped. In the first place his voice had really threatened to break. Then, it didn't seem very nice to be telling Aunt Kate that the only reason he'd come was that there wasn't anyone to take care of him at home. He'd *had* to come, really. That was the amount of it. Oh, he'd argued — he'd tried to persuade his father that he could take a job for the summer, for instance. But his father had only said, "There's plenty of work on the ranch, but it's good healthy outdoor work. You'll be in the sun and air — and get good regular meals. You'll like it out there," he'd said finally, "and you'll learn a lot." Tim didn't want to like it. All he wanted to do was stay home. That way, he figured, he could anyway *see* his mother every day, and sort of keep tabs on her. But now he was surprised to realize that he was beginning to like it here, after all.

Standing on the mountain path, his hands resting on his hipbones to ease the weight of his breathing, he told himself that he was liking it in spite of himself — and that he'd learned a lot already. He could saddle and bridle and harness a horse. He was riding pretty well with a saddle and he was learning to stick on bareback. He wasn't doing badly at mending fence and driving cattle. He knew the difference between grain and oats, and how much of each to feed. Looking down on the flowering meadows he thought to add that he'd learned the names of a dozen wildflowers. Aunt Kate knew them all, the way his mother knew them back east. "Here in Colorado," she told him, "they claim there's a wildflower for every day in the year." Tim loved best the tall blue lupin. He thought they were as beautiful as anything he'd ever seen in a garden, and he wished he could send some to his mother in the hospital. She'd really go for them! He could imagine her face when she looked at them. He imagined it so clearly that the homesick feeling began to creep over him, and he had to stop.

He forced his mind back to the present, and began to search the corral. Back of the barns an area was loosely fenced with post-and-rail fencing and there the saddle horses were kept. Aunt Kate had two she rode herself on alternating days, and if they were both in the corral it probably meant that she was in the house. He did want to tell her about what he had seen this morning!

She had sent him up to the high pasture to check on the salt licks. She was going in to town tomorrow and she wanted to know what she needed to order. The "licks" were big blocks of solid salt that might

9

have weighed fifty pounds apiece. They were put out in the pasture for the cattle. The horses licked them, too, and sometimes deer ventured out of the timber into the clearings to sneak a share of the salt. The high pasture was close to timberline. The air was very thin at that altitude, and a different sort of flower grew there: neither the tall blue lupin, nor the graceful Mariposa lily, nor even the scrubbier red Indian paintbrush. The flowers at that height were tiny and close to the earth, like Alpine flowers. Wildcats prowled there at times, and Aunt Kate had tried to describe for him their curious, pungent smell. "They're not apt to let you see 'em," she had said, "but if you catch that smell, look sharp!"

Tim had climbed slowly, stopping frequently to catch his breath. When he'd finally come out into the clearing, he'd sat down for a number of minutes, just feeling the warmth of the sun, and idly examining the blossoms at his feet, and not thinking about much of anything. When he could breathe naturally again, he stood up, and began to trace with his eyes the line of the barbed-wire fencing. "Check the fence while you're about it," Aunt Kate had said. Because of the presence of wild animals the fencing here was extra high, barbed at the top, and must always be kept in repair. Even at that, she told him, she usually lost a few calves each year. One thing Tim never hoped to learn was how to tell from the remains of a calf whether a wildcat or a timber wolf had got him. Aunt Kate could tell at once. But all she was able to say was, "One is an order of cat, and the other is an order of dog. And you know just as well as I do that cats and dogs don't go about things in the same way."

Tim's eyes had followed the fence about halfway around the pasture when some motion at the margin of his sight made him turn his head sharply. A great outcropping of rock, like a huge table of stone, loomed above the pasture at the far left, and turning toward it now, Tim saw that a wolf had come out to the edge of the rock and stood there looking down on him. The wolf was absolutely motionless now, but he must have just trotted out to the edge of the rock and it was the movement of his arrival that Tim had caught from the corner of his eye.

For a minute they simply looked at one another, and Tim was too surprised to be afraid. Outlined against the clear sky, the animal was like a statue, and Tim could only admire his stance, and his noble head with the alert, upstanding ears. But fear rose in him very quickly. It seemed to come up from his knees, which were suddenly so weak they trembled,

11

to clutch his stomach and turn it over, and then to close his throat. He needed to swallow, and couldn't. His throat was as dry as straw. His first conscious impulse was to turn and run. But could he? Would his legs work? And then maybe it was the wrong thing to do. Maybe if he ran, the wolf would run after him?

The rock was actually some distance from where Tim stood, but in the intense clarity of this air it appeared to be only a few yards away. He could see the animal's eyes as clearly as though they stood face to face in a small room. Somewhere Tim remembered he had heard that it wasn't a good idea to meet the eyes of a hostile beast. If he looked away, maybe the wolf would look away, too? If he could pretend he hadn't even seen him, the wolf might forget about him and go on about his own business, whatever it was. But it wasn't easy to look away. He wasn't sure it was possible. He felt compelled to go on looking into those strange, light eyes that were looking straight into his. It was almost as though he were being hypnotized. Did wolves always have yellow eyes? He'd never seen a wolf before, except in a picture, and that wasn't colored.

Tim couldn't possibly have said afterward how

long it was they both stood there, staring at each other. A minute? Five minutes? It seemed like an hour. But then his mind seemed slowly to unfreeze and begin to work. He remembered asking Aunt Kate if the wildcats and the timber wolves ever attacked people. "Might in the winter," she'd said. "If food's scarce and they get desperate. Wouldn't worry about it this time of year." So even if the wolf had got his scent, it was probably a calf he was really looking for. That made Tim's knees feel firmer. After a bit he was able to swallow, and then to shift his eyes and start to follow the line of the fence once more. He kept glancing back, though, to where the wolf still stood.

About the third time it seemed to him that the wolf didn't look quite so big. He didn't look much bigger than a good-sized dog. Maybe he was only a coyote, after all. They were smaller animals, and according to Aunt Kate, they were a cowardly breed. They preyed on gophers and prairie dogs, but they'd never attack anything much more than half their size. Still, there was something about this animal that wasn't the least bit cowardly. Aunt Kate described the coyote's gait as "slinking." This fine, upstanding creature was surely incapable of slink-

ing. Tim felt certain that he would always, as he was doing now, carry his head up and look the world straight in the eye.

A new thought came to Tim's mind. Maybe he was actually a dog? He'd have to be a German shepherd, and that in fact was exactly what he looked like. But then what was he doing way up here — where very few people came and no one at all lived? And then, those yellow eyes. Tim knew a good bit about dogs. His father was a vet and he'd taught Tim a lot. A good German shepherd had dark brown eyes. One that was less than purebred might run to light eyes, though.

By now he was so interested, and so curious, that

he'd lost most of his fear. Slowly he began to circle the pasture, looking for the blocks of salt and checking on their condition. The next time he raised his eyes to the rock, the wolf-dog had disappeared. Just the same, Tim went down the mountain in jig-time, and every now and then he paused to look back over his shoulder. Only when he reached the opening with its view of the valley and the ranch did he feel entirely safe.

Aunt Kate's two saddle horses were both in the corral, so there was every reason to suppose that Aunt Kate was in the house. She was most likely in the kitchen, talking to a ranch hand, or starting something for lunch. Occasionally outsiders drifted in: mountain climbers, or a party of "dudes" wanting to rent horses for the day. Aunt Kate had little use for the idle, but they brought in some ready cash, so she kept a second string of horses for rent, and she'd been known to put up lunches for a group of mountaineers.

When Tim burst into the kitchen, whose door was really the "front" door, he found her alone, at the stove. "Think you can stomach that stew again?" she asked him without even turning around. "Sure!" he said, "it was good." He was suddenly hungry, too. "Say, Aunt Kate," he began at once, "I saw a wolf in the high pasture. At least, I think it was a wolf —"

"Describe him!" she demanded, and now she turned around and fixed him with her keen, searching eyes.

"Well —" he started. "He was on that big rock — you know, the one that stands out like a table, flat on top? I — well, I kind of saw something move. You know, out of the corner of my eye?" She nodded. "How *big* is a wolf?" he paused to ask. "Pretty big when they're full grown," she told him. "Five feet long, more or less."

"Bigger than a German shepherd, then," he said. Aunt Kate's eyes narrowed. "Looked like a dog, did he?" she asked him. "That's right," he said. "He looked almost exactly like a big German shepherd. Except his eyes were too light. They were yellow, really, and that's not —"

"Lobo!" Aunt Kate said, interrupting him. "I call him Lobo," she explained, "for wolf, and because I'm danged if I know whether he's a wolf or a dog. Matter of fact," she said, "I'm not sure there's only one. Might be a pack of dogs gone wild and breeding up there at timberline. Might be breeding with wolves, far as that goes. I've seen him a number of times — if it's only the one." She stopped and laughed shortly. It was a funny, harsh sort of laugh, but it was the first time Tim had heard her laugh at all. "Came to me one night," she told him, "that it might be a ghost dog. You think of funny things sometimes, living up here alone. Walk out in these mountains at night when the moon's full and you can believe most anything."

Even standing in the bright, warm kitchen with the sun shining on the copper pots against the wall, and Aunt Kate right there beside the stove, it gave Tim an eerie feeling. It made his scalp prickle, and a little shiver ran down the back of his neck. "But who would it be the ghost of?" he asked a minute later.

"Some mountaineer's dog, I suppose," she said. "Had a feller come by here a few years back — stopped for a picnic lunch. It was too early to scale Snow Cap, and I told him so. Safer not to try it alone any time of year. But he was bent on it. Got buried in an avalanche. It was weeks before they found his body. Mid-June, as I recall. Never did lay eyes on the dog again."

"You mean he had a dog with him?" Tim asked.

"German shepherd," she said. "All alone except for that dog. Claimed the dog was a better climber than he was and he never went without him."

"Did they search for the dog? Do you think he got buried in the avalanche, too?"

"Doubt it," Aunt Kate said. "For one thing, he'd likely be lighter. And he'd be quicker, too." She shrugged now, as if she took no responsibility for what she was about to say, and Tim could make what he liked of it. "One of the searchers claimed he saw a dog, hanging around the scene. Thin as a rail, and half starved, but refusing to make up to anyone, and refusing to leave the place."

Tim had slipped off his knapsack that carried the coil of wire, the pinchers and the wire clippers, and now he sat down at the kitchen table. "How long ago was that?" he asked finally, out of a long silence.

"Hmm —" Aunt Kate considered. "Four years, maybe. I could figure it back. Let's see, that was the spring I got the palomino as a colt —"

Tim had stopped listening. Four years, maybe, he was thinking. Then it could be the same dog, waiting around for his master, haunting the scene of his death. He was imagining the dog's loss and his loneliness so intensely that his heart was shaken with sympathy. He could hardly wait to get up to the high pasture again.

2

Tɪᴍ waked the next morning sweating and feeling cold at the same time. He had waked straight out of a nightmare, and it was still more real than the room around him. It was as if he still felt the cold of the snow in his dream, and then the effort of running through it. He had been running to save his mother. But he hadn't been able to reach her. She was too far away.

Coming more fully awake, he moved to pull back the blankets he must have kicked off. Maybe it was the avalanche that had threatened his mother in the dream? Only that part wasn't clear. It was never clear in any of the dreams exactly what it was that threatened her. It was something different in each one, he thought. At least the places were all different, and the circumstances never the same. But the dreams were all alike in two respects: his mother was threatened, and he was helpless.

Once more the frightening question came into his mind: Were the dreams a kind of warning? Was his mother really in danger, as in fact he was really helpless? He might ask his father, of course. He might even ask Aunt Kate. But he decided against asking at all. Somehow just to put it into words would make it seem more real. It was better not even to think about it.

He got up and closed the window and began to dress very fast. The cold of the room made him think of the snow again, and then of the avalanche. And now all at once he remembered what it was that he wanted to think about. Lobo!

"You going in to town with me?" Aunt Kate asked him the minute he got down to the kitchen. She generally went in about twice a week, to pick up her mail at her post-office box, to market perhaps, possibly to stop at the feed dealer's or the blacksmith's. Tim enjoyed the trips to town. The only thing that bored him was the market, and he could skip that and go watch the blacksmith, for example. If he watched him a few more times, he figured he'd be able to shoe a horse himself. He'd already picked up some tips on mending harness, and one of his routine chores at the ranch was taking care of what he'd learned to call "tack," the bridles and harnesses and saddles that had their own orderly room in a section of the big barn.

Tim was interested in the town itself, too. It was a "ghost" town, a deserted silver-mining town. More than two thirds of the houses and stores were empty, and had been for many years. It kind of fascinated him to walk past the empty buildings, through the deserted streets, and imagine how it all used to be. But right now he had something else on his mind that interested him even more. "If it's O.K.," he said, "I guess I'll stay here. I'd kind of like to go up to the high pasture again —"

Aunt Kate nodded and went on stamping the letters she'd written, while Tim started in on his breakfast. She'd gone through the catalogues the night before and made out her orders. Most of her buying had to be done by mail, and almost all her correspondence was with the mail-order houses. Tim had written a couple of postcards to friends back home and a letter to his mother. He fished them out of the hip pocket of his dungarees now and added them to the pile she was stuffing into one pouch of her saddlebags. She used the saddlebags as most women use a purse or a marketing bag, and she seldom went anywhere without them.

"I've got my list," she said. "Now, anything you want from the five-and-dime?" He couldn't think of a thing, and he was getting impatient for her to

be off. Buck had already hitched up the horses and the buckboard was waiting by the first barn. Still Aunt Kate hesitated. "If Shep comes by," she said, "try to trade him the pinto pony. He's got his eye on Juanita, but I'm not letting her go." Tim's heart sank. Hadn't she listened to him at all? And would he have to stay at the house, after all? He began to figure. He could leave a note. Or he could round up one of the ranch hands, maybe, and leave the transaction to him. But his conscience troubled him. "Trip's going to be working on the cattle guard," he said. Aunt Kate had to drive past the cattle guard in order to get off her property and out onto the town road. She'd have to see Trip if he was where he'd said he would be. "If you'd — er — mention to him about Shep and the pinto," Tim said. "I mean — in case I miss Shep," he added, "going up to the high pasture — " Aunt Kate gave him a searching look. "You won't learn to trade any younger," she told him. "And Shep's a good man to learn on. But I'll speak to Trip if you insist. You got that ghost-dog on your mind?" she asked. Tim had learned by now that Aunt Kate was kinder than she sounded. She was just sort of — well, matter-of-fact. And now at last she was ready to go.

He watched the buckboard take off down the

road, with Dexter and Sinister stepping high, and gleaming like burnished copper in the sun. It was a sight he always enjoyed. And now he'd got so he kind of liked to look at Aunt Kate, too, sitting up there so tiny under her shawl and handling the big horses so surely. He guessed Aunt Kate could handle most anything. She was a funny sort of person to feel *fond* of, though. Tim didn't suppose she was fond of anyone — except maybe old Mac. Stepping back into the kitchen, he stooped and patted the old collie on the floor by the stove. Mac was usually near the stove until the sun got high, about noon, and flooded the kitchen steps with warmth. Then he'd get up, stiffly, and go outside to lie in the sun until it began to wester and go down. Mac was the only idle member of the establishment. "Lazy critter!" Aunt Kate would often say, but she always said it in a gentle sort of voice that Tim never heard otherwise. And she usually added: "He's earned it! Best cattle dog in the county, for nigh on fifteen years. I ought to get a young 'un to start training," she'd sometimes add. But Tim guessed she never would — or not until old Mac died.

He reached his knapsack down from its hook on the kitchen wall, got a tin of Mac's dog food from the pantry shelf and began to ransack the table drawer for an old can opener. Maybe a tin plate, too, he thought — an old one that could be left in the pasture and not be missed. When he'd put them all into his pack, he made himself a peanut-butter sandwich. On second thought he added some jelly, and then he filled Aunt Kate's canteen with milk. Now he was ready. At the last minute he thought to write a note to stick onto the screen door with "Shep" penciled on the outside, just in case.

Personally, he considered, as he started up the path toward the high pasture, he'd sooner give up Juanita any day than the pinto colt, or nearly any of the others. She was a big dapple gray, or blue roan, that looked to Tim more like a cart horse than his idea of a saddle horse. But if Aunt Kate valued her, and Shep wanted her, then Tim guessed he had a long way to go before he'd be any judge of horses. That was one of the things Aunt Kate had been very nice about, though. "You've got a sense of style," she'd told him. "It's just — there's more to it than that. But you can only get it with experience."

The sun was hot already although it would be a couple of hours till noon. Halfway across the meadow Tim shrugged out of his sweater and tied it by the sleeves around his middle. Even when he got into the trees it would be a hot climb. He'd never seen such weather before. Day after day the sun shone in a brilliant blue sky. Occasionally there'd be a shower, but the rain never lasted long. The clouds would come up so fast you could hardly get to shelter. He'd got caught in a couple of thunderstorms, too, and they were violent. He'd never been afraid of lightning, but he didn't like it here in the mountains. The horses were afraid of it, and sometimes a horse was struck. Wet hide seemed to draw the lightning, and Tim figured he'd dismount fast if he ever got caught while riding. But the storms were as brief as the showers, and he'd yet to see a day that wasn't mainly clear.

Eager as he was to reach the high pasture, he had to stop frequently. Gooseberries grew along the trail, and he sat down once or twice to pick and eat some. They were sour, but they were good for thirst. He was glad he'd thought to bring the milk. Aunt Kate never climbed without her canteen, although part way up the mountain there was a rushing stream that crossed the trail. "No better water in the world," Aunt Kate had told him, "if some animal hasn't died in it just above." Tim wanted to know how you could tell. "You can't," she said simply. So he leapt the stream without pausing to drink.

When he finally came out into the clearing that was the high pasture, he looked at once to the big rock. From across the breadth of the pasture he could see more of its flat top. It was a huge surface. You could build a house on it and still have room to move around outside. But it was bare and unoccupied now. Tim sat down and uncorked the canteen, and when he'd started to breathe more easily, he drank a little of the milk, tilting back his head and still keeping his eyes on the rock. Perhaps he'd have to approach the rock so that Lobo could get his scent? There wasn't much wind stirring, but he wet his finger and held it up anyway. No wind at all, he decided. For a few minutes he sat on, considering his approach. If Lobo *did* appear, then how should he go about attracting him? To get the horses down he rattled a tin of grain. His instinct today had been to bring food as lure — but maybe Lobo wasn't hungry? He must have learned to rustle his own grub or he wouldn't be still alive — let alone looking so far from the half-starved dog the searcher had described. Tim was assuming now that Lobo was the mountaineer's dog. If it was a guess, he had ceased to question it. If it was a hunch, it was such a strong one that he was determined to play it.

It might seem a little crazy to someone who didn't know about the cemetery dog back home. Tim's father had told him about the dog who lived in the cemetery, and then he'd taken Tim there to see for himself. According to the men who tended the place, and clipped the grass on the graves, the dog had been there more than three years at the time Tim went and saw him — a small black cocker spaniel whose coat was all tangles and knots. He never left the grave of his master except to steal out at night and raid the neighborhood garbage pails. If a cocker spaniel could live like that, how could anyone doubt a great-hearted shepherd?

Tim opened the tin of meat and dumped the contents onto the pie plate he'd brought. Then he got to his feet and started slowly across the clearing. Without exactly admitting to himself that he had any fear left at all, he half-consciously felt for the sheathed knife attached to his belt. His father had given it to him when he left, and Tim kept it on his belt at all times. He'd never seriously imagined using it for anything but whittling a stick or cleaning a fish, but it gave him a vague sense of security, as if he was prepared for anything.

3

ABOUT where he'd been standing the day before,
Tim stopped. Suppose he were to whistle? He decided against it, though. Let Lobo get his scent, if
he happened to be where he could. Let him just
appear of his own accord, again, he thought, and
just take another good look. That way, he reasoned,
the dog wouldn't take alarm. Maybe, Tim told himself next, he'd have to come here day after day, until
Lobo got used to him. It was kind of a discouraging
thought because Patience wasn't exactly his middle
name, and he knew it. He shifted his weight from
one foot to the other, and finally he gave up and sat
down. After a bit he plucked a wide blade of grass,
the kind you could put between your thumbs and
use for a whistle. He knew how to whistle with two
fingers in his mouth, as well, and that made a real
strong, carrying whistle. He began to think about
the mountaineer. He began to wonder how he used
to call the dog. Maybe he'd had one of those high-
pitched real whistles that only a dog could hear?
Tim's father had one of them, but that was two
thousand miles back east.

Tim wiped his sweating face with the sleeve of his shirt, and tried another swallow of milk. "Come on, Lobo!" he said. It must be about noon, he figured, and time to crack out his sandwich. He got it out of the knapsack and peeled off the wax paper. It smelled good, and he was glad he'd added the jelly. He took a big bite and then, almost automatically, he raised his eyes to the rock again. For a second he thought he was going to choke. Lobo had come out on the rock and stood there looking down at him. Tim grabbed the canteen and without shifting his eyes from the dog he took a good swallow of the milk. "Lobo!" he said then, but softly, almost under his breath. Now he had no doubt at all. This was a dog, and a good one. Even his eyes looked different today. They were light — a little too light — but they weren't really yellow. It must have been the sun, he thought now. The sun must have been straight in his eyes yesterday. And then, he decided fairly, he'd been scared. He'd *expected* a wolf, so naturally he'd *seen* a wolf. The knowledge came so simply that he wasn't even aware of having learned something.

"Good boy!" he said, trying to make his voice carry now. "Good fella!" He picked up the plate from beside him on the grass and held it out.

31

"Food!" he said. "Are you hungry?" He wasn't sure whether the dog could hear him or not, but still he went on talking. "I like you, boy!" he said. "You're great. Why don't you come on down and let's make friends? You need a friend," he said, "same as I do." The dog just kept looking at him. "You can trust me," Tim said next. "I only want to give you something to eat — " He shook the plate around a bit, but of course it didn't rattle like grain. And Lobo wasn't a horse. He wasn't even, any longer, exactly a tame dog.

Tim was remembering the tragic story that Aunt Kate had told him, and his heart was stirred all over again. Lobo had lived for four years, maybe, like a wild animal, sleeping in some cave in the rocks, killing his own food and avoiding all human contact while he waited for his own, one person to come back to life again. It was the dog's loss and his loneliness that had drawn Tim to him like a magnet, and now he was imagining it all over again. Well, actually he didn't have to imagine, he *knew* how Lobo felt. He was feeling it so intensely at this moment that his eyes smarted with the beginning of tears. But why were the feelings so familiar and as if they were his own? The answer came like a brilliant memory that forced everything else from his

mind. He wasn't really seeing Lobo now, although he hadn't moved his eyes. He was seeing his mother lying in bed in that hospital room.

It was the day he'd gone to say good-bye before leaving. They hadn't stayed very long. His father had got up to leave before Tim was ready to go. When they got outside the room, his father stopped to speak to a nurse. It was then that Tim sneaked back, to say good-bye again by himself. He wished he hadn't. His mother's eyes were closed, and she looked terribly white, and frighteningly still. The soundless door had swung shut behind him, and in the fearful silence of the room it took all his courage to speak. His mother didn't hear him, and then in a clutch of panic he had backed out of the room. He bumped into his father who was standing alone now in the hall. "Is Mother — is she — ?" He had to ask and he couldn't ask. But he guessed his father understood. He put his hand on Tim's shoulder. "I expect she's asleep," he said. "She was tired today. That's why we had to leave." He took Tim down to the hospital cafeteria and got him some black coffee. It was the first time Tim had ever had coffee, and he didn't like it much, after all.

He'd wished at the time that he hadn't gone back, and he'd wished it ever since. He should have left while his mother's eyes were still open, and she was smiling at him. He had to shake himself to get rid of the memory, and then he had to refocus his eyes. Lobo was still there — and what a handsome fellow he was! As if his life depended on it, Tim fixed his attention on the dog.

Big-boned and deep-chested, he was a powerful animal. He hadn't Tim's favorite coloring for a shepherd. He liked best what was known as black and silver, although the "silver" was actually closer to a light sand color. A black-saddled shepherd with light legs and light face markings was his idea of a really sharp-looking dog. Lobo was all one color. He was what you might call brindled, Tim thought. That was why it had been so easy to mistake him for a wolf. But now Tim realized that a wolf would have a broader head and smaller ears. Only a well-bred dog would have such a fine head, and such magnificent upstanding ears.

On a sudden impulse Tim whistled, just an ordinary two-note whistle. At once Lobo cocked his head, in the unmistakable response of a dog, and a dog who was accustomed to people. Immediately after, he righted his head and seemed to pretend he hadn't moved, or made any sign. Tim laughed. "It's too late to fool me, boy," he said. "You gave yourself away for sure that time. Come on, now. Let's make friends? O.K.?" The dog continued to stand like a statue, and now he appeared to be looking past Tim, as though he didn't exist. A minute later he turned and trotted back across the rock and out of sight.

It was Tim's first look at his hindquarters. His rear angulation was good, and he had a fine, heavy straight-hanging tail. He was a pure-bred shepherd, all right, Tim decided. Except for his eyes being a little too light, you couldn't fault him. But he was gone, and Tim made the guess that he wouldn't appear again today no matter how long he might wait. Now if he could just find a good place to leave the dog food, he thought.

At the spot where the big rock overhung the fence, the fence was less high. The posts connected with the first bulge of the outcropping rock, and couldn't have gone any higher. Tim estimated them to be little more than three feet high at that point. Carrying the plate of food, he started to approach the rock, studying its stony surface as he walked. If there were crevices or small ledges, he might plant the tin plate on one of them. He guessed the dog, or any animal, could come down the face of the rock if he picked himself an angled route. He suspected it might be the way the wildcats got into the pasture. If it was only a three-foot drop from the top of the posts, it would be a lot easier than jumping the five-foot fence that enclosed the rest of the pasture.

As he got closer, Tim thought he could make out a zigzag sort of path down the rock. It was a faint, interrupted line, but it was darker than the surrounding stone, as though from recurrent moisture. It was probably the course the rain took, he reasoned, and then maybe with the continual tracking of animals it had deepened. He doubted if a person could scale by it, even with the occasional projections that might provide a toe hold. But for the small, sure feet of animals he thought it would just about do, and he began to search for a ledge within his reach.

He walked the breadth of the rock — four post lengths — scanning the rock's surface minutely as he did so. Nothing looked wide enough to balance the tin pie plate. He'd have to dump the dog food right on the rock, and when he'd found a likely-looking projection close to one of the posts, he tested the barbed wire with his weight. Using the wire like steps, he climbed to the top of the fence, and resting one knee against the post, he scooped out the meat and dropped it onto the narrow ledge. It pleased him to think of Lobo getting the scent of his hands on the food.

Tomorrow, he thought hopefully — or the next day — he might leave the dog food down in the pasture. With that in mind, he decided to leave the tin plate, and he propped it securely against the base of the fence post. If he could get Lobo used to eating like a house dog again, it might be the beginning of getting him used to living like a house dog once more.

Tim was a long way from being able to tell time by the sun as accurately as Aunt Kate could, or even Buck. But he liked to try. Now he guessed it might be about ten minutes past one. Aunt Kate should be back. And she might have some mail for him! There might be a letter from his mother, for instance, with any luck. In any case, he could really look forward to eating something more hearty than a sandwich. Hands on hips, he started off.

When he'd recrossed the clearing to where the trail plunged down the mountain through the tall, crowding trees, he paused to look back toward the rock again. A little back from the edge, but in plain view, Lobo stood outlined against the sky. He might have been there the whole time, but just out of sight from below. He must have been watching Tim's

progress across the pasture. Tim took it for such a good sign of the dog's interest that he was encouraged to raise his arm and wave. "I'll be back!" he called out, before starting down the trail. "I'll be back tomorrow!" If Aunt Kate had brought the salt licks from town, he could ride one of the pack horses up the next day.

From the opening at the end of the trail, the ranch looked sleepy down there in the sun. The saddle horses were all in the corral, but Tim couldn't tell from here whether or not the buckboard had come back. It was kept in the second barn. Dexter and Sinister would be in their stalls, getting their noontime grain, if they'd returned from town. Tim was really hungry by now, and he sprinted the last stretch to the meadow.

His penciled note was still in the crack of the screen door, so Shep hadn't come by, after all. Tim took down the scrap of paper and crumpled it in his hand as he pushed through the door. The kitchen was empty. There were no bundles on the counters, and nothing was cooking on the stove. Aunt Kate must have waited for the second mail to be sorted and put in the boxes. Or maybe she'd met another rancher at the feed store. She might have run into Shep, for instance, and they might have got into a long-winded talk. Tim had to smile to himself. He'd listened to them "trading" for an hour or more and then keeping their own horses in the end. He began to search the pantry shelves for something that would be easy to heat up.

Thinking about something to heat up, he remembered that he ought to shake down the stove, and put in more coal. As he stepped back across the kitchen, it came to him that old Mac wasn't in his usual place on the floor by the stove. And if he'd been out on the steps, in the sun, Tim would have seen him as he came by. He never passed the old dog without speaking to him, or stooping to pat him, and fondle his ears. And Mac always lifted his head, and thumped his tail a few times in greeting.

Tim went to the door and looked out. No sign of Mac, and that was strange. Just at first Tim was only surprised and curious. Where could the dog be? In all the time Tim had been here he'd hardly ever known Mac to vary his short route from the stove to the steps, and back again. He sometimes went down to the brook, but never any farther than that. Tim pushed the swinging screen door and stepped outside again. He scanned the meadow, as far as the brook. By now he was beginning to feel anxious. He turned and looked down the road.

After a second he shaded his eyes, in order to see more clearly. The movement he'd caught was old Mac, all right, walking way down the road, moving very stiffly and slowly, and keeping to the grass at one side. He'd got quite a way, although he looked as if he could barely move.

At one and the same time Tim was relieved to see him at all, and alarmed to see him going down the road where he'd never gone before. What had got into him? What was he after? Maybe something had happened, and Mac's instinct had told him about it? Maybe Aunt Kate had had an accident, for instance? Overturned in the buckboard, maybe? Tim figured it must have something to do with Aunt Kate. She was the center of Mac's world. A sort of panic was rising in Tim, and he realized that his heart had begun to thump. Without stopping to think about it, he put two fingers in the corners of his mouth and whistled a piercing blast.

The whistle had reached Mac's ears. Tim could see him pause, try to turn, and then totter. In the next second Tim saw with horror that the old dog was sinking to the ground. He told himself that he shouldn't have whistled. He shouldn't have startled old Mac. But it was too late to worry about that, and Tim set off at a dead run down the road.

4

Tim's heart was really racing by the time he'd got
down the road to where old Mac lay. He was pant-
ing with exertion and anxiety both. He was close to
choking with the dust he'd kicked up, and he was
sweating from the heat of the midday sun. But he
was only half conscious of his own condition in his
overwhelming concern for Mac. He wondered how
much the old dog weighed. Would he be able to
pick him up? Would he be be able to carry him, if
that should be necessary? At one time in Mac's life
he must have weighed as much as Tim himself. He
must have been a well-muscled dog, strong of bone
and heavily coated. His muscles were slack now
from little use, and his coat had thinned badly. He
was lean, and kind of pathetic, with bare places in
his fur.

Tim leaned over and looked down at him. The
dog's eyes were closed. Was he breathing or not?
He looked to be motionless. Resting his hands on
his hipbones, Tim stood for a couple of seconds just

looking down on old Mac. His mind was working, though. He'd gone with his father on his calls sometimes. And once or twice by the time they got there the dog or cat was already beyond help. Distemper, or hit by a car, and the vet arrived to find the animal dead.

He knelt down beside old Mac and put his head against the dog's chest the way he'd seen his father do when there was any doubt in his mind. He could pick up no movement or beat. But perhaps this was his own ignorance? Perhaps he didn't know how to listen, or exactly where. If the pulse of life was very faint it might take someone skilled to catch it. He wished he had a stethoscope. He sat back on his heels and said, "Mac? Mac, are you there, old boy? Open your eyes!" he urged him. "Look at me, Mac!" he begged him. He stared at the closed eyes. Still he wasn't convinced. It might be a heat stroke. He'd heard of heat prostration with people, anyway. If he could get the dog back to the house — if he could settle him down beside the stove again, in the warmth — then he might revive. It sounded kind of nutty, but he was sure he'd heard that if a person got heat prostration you were supposed to wrap him in a blanket. He resettled himself on the ground in a strong, lifting position. Then he put one arm under

Mac's head, and the other one under his haunches. Now, maybe, he could get him up.

It took three tries, but then he had Mac in his arms and was able to struggle to his feet, holding the dog. Now if he could just get him across his shoulders. Aunt Kate had taught him the value of a pack on your back. You could carry more weight on your shoulders that you could in your arms. It was the principle of the yoke. This was harder to do, and Tim nearly fell down in the shift. But finally he had the dog like a sheep across his shoulders, and holding his front legs in one hand, his rear legs in the other, he started slowly back toward the house.

He hoped Aunt Kate wouldn't come along right now. He wanted to get Mac into the house, in his accustomed place, and he even hoped to revive him before she returned. Perhaps Mac had only fainted, but he certainly was dead weight. Tim had to stop a number of times, and once he shifted Mac's weight a little. As he approached the house it occurred to him that it might be better to go around to the bunkhouse back of the barns. If Buck were there he might be of some help. In any case, Tim thought, it would be better if Aunt Kate didn't see old Mac until he'd come to.

The bunkhouse was empty, and smelled of freshly

cooked bacon. Buck must have had his lunch and gone out again. Trip had a family and his own house down the road. Tim decided to put Mac down on Buck's bed, and then to pull a blanket over him, only leaving his head out. He wished he knew what to do next. Should he try to get some water into him? Or maybe some milk? But just then he heard what he was pretty sure was the rattle of the buckboard coming in to the barn. He gave Mac a reassuring pat. "It's all right, boy!" he said. "I'll be back," and hastily wiping the sweat from his face with the back of his arm, he went out to meet Aunt Kate.

"Waited for the second mail," she said. "Thought those cinches I ordered ought to turn up, and they did." She was taking the bundles from the back of the buckboard and setting them down on the barn floor. Tim put out his hand to touch Dexter's nose as he went by him and then, to his own surprise, he put his head against the horse's head and just stood there for a minute. A strange sort of weakness had suddenly come over him and he was afraid there were tears in his eyes. He guessed old Mac was pretty heavy, after all. But he had to pull himself together. "Want me to unharness?" he asked, and was relieved to hear his own voice sounding natural.

"Wish you would," Aunt Kate said. "And I'll go in and rustle us some grub." Tim began to unfasten the harness. He was glad Aunt Kate wasn't looking at him. His hands seemed to be trembling a little, and his fingers were clumsy. "Rodeo in town next week," she said just before gathering up her saddle bags. "Want me to enter the team again," she said. "How d'you like to ride in the parade? Most of the kids do." Well, she'd distracted him, all right. "Sure — " he said. "If you think I can do O.K." Aunt Kate grunted. "You'll see a lot worse," she told him. "All the summer folks turn out. Nothing to it but keeping one leg on either side of the horse. Who'd you like to ride?" Tim had already begun to think about that. He'd had, in fact, a swift, brilliant picture of himself up on the palomino. It was pure wishful thinking, and he knew it. The palomino was a stallion. But the picture had just sort of come into his mind. "Plenty of time to think about it," Aunt Kate said now, and with that she strode out of the barn with her swinging step that made the saddle bags swing.

Tim's hands had steadied now, and he was more or less all right. Still he was glad to be left alone. He was working hastily, though, as if he couldn't wait to finish and get back to old Mac. And that was funny, because at the same time he dreaded going to the bunkhouse again. When he'd got the horses out of harness, and they'd trotted into their stalls, he hurriedly scooped up some grain and dumped it into their feed boxes. Then he hung up the tack with only a careless swipe at the sweaty reins and the bits that were sticky with saliva. He ran his damp hands down the sides of his dungarees, and took a deep breath that shook a little.

At the door to the bunkhouse he slowed down and stepped softly into the room. Old Mac hadn't stirred. He was in exactly the position Tim had left him, with the blanket up to his ears and his head limp on the bed. "Mac?" he said, moving quietly across the floor. "Maccy, old boy?" If only he'd lift his head, and thump his tail. If he'd even open his eyes! Tim got down on his knees beside the bunk, and once again he put his head to the old dog's chest, moving the blanket back a little in order to do so. Did he imagine it, or was old Mac's body less warm than it had been? He'd felt like a warm fur blanket across Tim's shoulders. Tim remembered that he'd seen his father massage a dog's heart. He didn't think it had ever worked, but it must be something worth trying or why had his father tried? Tim reached his hand down under the blanket, under

Mac's chest. The next instant he withdrew it in a sort of horror. His hand was covered with fleas, dozens of them. And now he saw that the blanket was swarming with them, too. This was something he'd never seen or heard of, but it came to him what it meant. The fleas were leaving Mac's body, and Tim's instinct told him why. Shaking his hand and rubbing it against the blanket, he was swept with a sense of loathing, a strange sort of fear, and at the same time he was overcome with grief. Now the tears really came. Tim dropped his head on the hard edge of the bunk and shook all over with his crying.

When he was able to control himself and think again he began to worry about Aunt Kate. What should he say to her? How could he tell her? And what would she do? It was hard to imagine, and he gave up trying and forced himself, instead, to get on with it. He wouldn't go straight to the house, though. He'd go around by the barn and soak his head in the watering trough first.

He'd hardly stepped across the threshold into the kitchen before Aunt Kate said, "Where's Mac?" He had to make himself meet her eyes. It was even harder to make himself speak. "I — I think he's — d-dead," he stammered. "What do you mean you 'think'?" she rapped out in a fast, tight sort of voice. "Don't you know the difference between life and death? Where is he?"

"He's in the bunkhouse," Tim told her. "On Buck's bed. You — you want me to — " he was starting to ask her if she wanted him to go with her, but she'd got out the door already, and he guessed he wasn't supposed to follow.

He felt tired all over and still he couldn't sit down. He kept pacing up and down the room. He could hear Aunt Kate saying, "Don't you know the difference between life and death?" The thing was, he hadn't really wanted to know. But now he knew, all right. He knew the way he'd never known before. He'd seen animals who had died, sure. But they'd never been anyone he knew. It was entirely different when it was someone you knew. Death was real when it happened to someone you knew. It was as real as life! Was this one of the things he'd been sent out here to learn? O.K., he thought angrily. So he'd learned. And he just hoped his father knew how much he hated it! He hoped he'd never learn any more, too!

His mind went right on, though. He couldn't stop it. Suppose, he thought next, it happened to a *person* you knew? Suppose it was his mother, for example? Somehow, this morning in the pasture, he'd been able to switch off his mind. Finally, anyway, he'd been able to switch it off, and turn it on to the dog. But now he was right up against it. Now he admitted to himself that he'd thought his mother was dead. That was what he'd thought in the silent hospital room. That was what he had feared, so terribly that he couldn't even say it. So now he'd admitted it. Now he'd said it to himself. So now he could think about Aunt Kate. He certainly didn't want her to die! But she was infinitely older than his mother, for example.

He kept moving around the kitchen looking at things without seeing them. When the pressure cooker began to hiss on the stove, it was a minute before he really heard it. Then he went over and pushed it to the back of the stove. Everything had to be cooked under pressure at this altitude. Otherwise you could cook something most of the day and it still wouldn't be done. That was because the boiling point of water was so low. He'd learned about that in school. That was one thing, anyway, that Aunt Kate didn't have to explain to him. It gave him a brief satisfaction to remember it.

When Aunt Kate came back, she went straight to the stove to check on the pressure cooker. "I just

moved it," he told her. "About — about two minutes ago, I guess." She glanced at the clock above
the sink. "How'd he get to the bunkhouse?" she
asked then. "I carried him," Tim said. "I thought
— well, I figured — " She interrupted him. "Just
tell me what happened," she said. "He was going
down the road," Tim said. Aunt Kate was looking
at him now. She nodded. "Going after me," she
said. "Go on!" she prodded him. "I whistled," Tim
told her, "and he started to turn around. Then he —
he just sort of fell down." This was hard but he had
to say it. "Maybe if I hadn't whistled — I mean,
maybe I — " Aunt Kate shook her head impatiently.
"He was on the way out," she said, "and he knew it."
It gave Tim a certain relief. He hadn't finished,
though, and the worst part was still to come. "But
if I'd been here when he set off — " he said. "I
mean, I was up in the high pasture. When I got
down, Mac wasn't here. But if I'd been here," he
said again, "I might have stopped him." And now
he'd expressed the burden of his guilt, and in a sudden collapsing motion he sat down on the nearest
chair. Maybe he ought to add that he'd left the note
for Shep — that he hadn't just skipped out on everything? But there didn't seem to be any blame in
Aunt Kate's face. She was kind of smiling. It was an

53

odd, a grim sort of smile. And then she spoke. "You think you can stop death?" she said. It wasn't exactly a question, and it certainly didn't need an answer. She glanced at the clock again. "You got any appetite?" she asked him. He wasn't sure.

5

Tim waked the next morning to the familiar smell
of bacon cooking. It was coming up through the
floor boards from the kitchen under his room. He
usually woke to this smell, and it usually got him
right up. Out here he rose a lot earlier than he ever
had at home, but still he was never ahead of Aunt
Kate. But this morning felt different, though he
couldn't remember straight off why that was. He
hunched down farther under the blankets and
waited to find out. No matter how hot the days
might be, they chilled off fast when the sun went
down, and the early mornings were still cold. Tim
liked the coolness on his face and the warmth of the
blankets on his body at the same time. And now, all
at once, he knew what it was that had been troubling at the back of his mind. The sharp, painful
memory of old Mac wrapped up in the blanket had
come abruptly back, and he had to think about it
again.

He began to go slowly over the whole thing, from the beginning, and until he got right up to where they'd buried old Mac that afternoon. Tim thought he'd never forget Aunt Kate lowering Mac into the grave that Buck and he had dug, under her directions, down by the brook. She kept talking the whole time in a rambling sort of way that wasn't the least like her, telling how Mac had always loved the brook, how he used to play there as a puppy, splashing into the water and trying to catch a trout. Buck had kept digging in a fast, nervous sort of way. Well, Tim was pretty nervous, too. He wasn't exactly worried — or not about anyone but himself. He felt as if he might start crying again, and he never let himself cry in front of anyone else. He certainly wasn't nervous about Aunt Kate. It seemed to come to him that she had to act this way, and it was all right.

Thinking about it now, he decided it was more than all right, it was nice — telling about how Mac was, and all the things he used to do. It was a kind of *remembering* — that's what it was. He guessed it was necessary, and he thought it was nice. It almost made him feel as if he'd known Mac as a puppy himself. After a bit he found himself smiling, picturing the big-pawed clumsy puppy trying to catch a trout. And now he began to feel better and was able to get out of bed.

While he washed and got into his clothes he thought about the day that was waiting for him to begin it. He'd go up to the high pasture again. With any luck he'd be able to ride up. "I'll get in some more practice," he told himself, remembering the rodeo. He took the steep stairs three at a time and landed in the kitchen with a thud. "You get the salt licks, Aunt Kate?" he asked her immediately. "Gee, that smells good," he added in the next breath. "I'm starved."

Aunt Kate said, "Good morning," which made him feel rude since he hadn't said it to her. "You washed?" she asked him next, and *that* made him feel about six years old. It was maddening! But the kitchen was flooded with sunshine, and now he saw that there were two eggs in the pan along with the bacon. There weren't any hens on the ranch, and Aunt Kate didn't often buy eggs. She must have got some yesterday because she knew how much he liked them. All in all he began to calm down. "Clean as a whistle," he told her cheerfully. "If you got the salt," he said then, "I'll take it up to the high pasture after breakfast." She was picking up the eggs with a pancake turner. "You better pack

Cheyenne," she told him. So she'd got the salt, all right. "Trip was working him yesterday," she went on, "so he ought to be tractable. Bimbo's been idle more'n a week and likely feeling his oats." Tim felt as if he could handle anything right now and would rather like the experience. "What could a *pack* horse do?" he asked. "Buck off the pack, including you," she told him. "Or brush you off against a tree," she added, "and that can be worse. No quicker way to break a knee." He mentally settled for Cheyenne, and began to think about his plan for the day.

When they'd finished breakfast, and Aunt Kate was busy at the sink, Tim got down his knapsack and managed to slip in another can of dog food. There was almost half a case of Mac's food left, and Aunt Kate would be the first person to want it used. She didn't like anything wasted. But he didn't think it would be very nice to bring it to her attention just now. For the same reason he said nothing about Lobo, although his mind was so full of the dog that he almost had to bite his tongue a couple of times.

It was a lot easier riding than climbing. Secretly, Tim didn't really call this riding. His idea of riding was to be up on a spirited horse going at a fast trot, or better still a canter or gallop. If the horse wanted to side-step and shy — at a tumbleweed blowing across the road, for example — that was all right with Tim. A couple of times he'd had a horse rear with him. He'd just managed to stay on, but even at the time it was exciting. Afterwards he thought it was great, and he only wished someone had seen him, with the horse standing straight up and pawing the air, and himself down fast in the saddle like a jockey pulling up at the finish of a race. That was really riding but this, he considered, was just a way of getting from one place to another.

But the air was cool under the trees and he kept noticing things he'd never taken the time to notice before. Under the aspens, for instance, the air was different from what it was under the dark firs. The trunks of the aspens were a light, greenish color. They were so light they reminded him of the birches back home. But instead of being white the aspens' bark was a soft green. He tried to think how he'd describe them to his mother. It was as though their color tinted the air around them, and riding through a grove of them was like moving through green air, or swimming under water. He'd especially like to write his mother about the columbines that seemed to grow most thickly in an aspen grove. They were the Colorado state flower and he'd never seen them, back East, so big and so pretty. Here they were almost the color of violets, and they seemed to look best of all against the pale green trunks of the aspens.

When they got to where the stream crossed the trail, Cheyenne stopped and tried to get his head down to drink. Maybe, Tim thought, an animal had an instinct that a person didn't have? So maybe the water was unpolluted, and O.K., and he ought to let the horse have a drink. He wasn't sure, though, so he pulled him up short, and then kicked him on. A little later, in order to make up, he let Cheyenne stop and eat the head off a thistle. Personally, Tim told himself, he'd as soon eat a prickly cactus. There wasn't much difference, except for the color. And that was funny, he thought now. Could a horse tell one color from another? They always spotted the purple thistles, and it was sometimes all he could do to get them past one. He'd have to ask Aunt Kate about that.

When the trail got really steep, Cheyenne stopped and let out a sigh. Tim prodded him with his heels. "Come on!" he said sternly. "You can climb as well as I can, or better." The horse continued to stand with his feet planted, and now he sighed again, more deeply. This time Tim could feel the air go out of him. It was like a balloon going down. It was a danger signal, too, and Tim was taking no chances on getting off in the usual way, with his full weight, however briefly, hanging on the one stirrup. He kicked his left foot free, swung his right foot over the pummel, and slid to the ground fast. Then he picked up the stirrup leather, raised the saddle flap under it, and shoved in his hand. Sure enough, the cinch was so loose he could get his whole hand under it. "Hey, you bum!" he said. But really it was his own fault, and he knew it. Swelling up while being saddled was a trick any horse would pull. You had to leave him for a few minutes, while he relaxed and unswelled, and then go back and tighten the cinch. Otherwise the saddle could turn under you when you least expected it, and give you a nasty spill. Tim had forgotten to recinch today. Now he really tightened it, bracing one foot against the horse as he pulled up the slack, the way he'd seen Buck do. "Let that be a lesson to you!" he said. At that the horse turned his head way around and looked straight back at him. It was exactly as if he was saying, "You talking to me, or yourself?" Tim burst out laughing. "O.K.," he said, "you win. It was my own dumb fault." He gave Cheyenne's nose a friendly shove, gathered up the reins and remounted.

The horse plodded on patiently until he got in sight of the pasture. Then he really picked up his feet and began to trot. Figured he was in for some good grazing, no doubt. Tim sat a little straighter, and shortened the reins. He was already looking in the direction of the rock, and he scanned it the minute they trotted into the clearing. It was bare. Tim dismounted and threw the reins over Cheyenne's head to drop on the ground in front of him. Most western horses were trained to stand if their reins were down, and all of Aunt Kate's certainly were. All Tim wanted to do was cross the pasture at once, to see if yesterday's food had been eaten, and then to put down some more food. But he had a job to do first. The wrapped blocks of salt hung one at either side of Cheyenne's belly, just back of the saddle. Tim started to loosen the pack, and then he did a double take. No sense trying to lug them across the pasture himself. Cheyenne could do it a lot more easily. He picked up the reins again and started to walk, leading the horse.

When he'd deposited the licks at the opposite ends of the pasture, he led the horse back toward the trail, against the margin of the trees. He wanted to be alone in the pasture, just the way he'd been before. If anything was any different, he was afraid

Lobo might take alarm — or perhaps not recognize him. He had to build up the dog's trust, and he wanted to establish a relationship with him. He left Cheyenne with his head down, nibbling the close, sweet grass. Even if the horse weren't trained to stand, he'd be bound to stay with the good grazing.

The first thing Tim did was to climb the fence post again and check on the ledge where he'd left the food yesterday. There wasn't a trace of it. Of course that didn't prove it was Lobo who'd got it, but Tim was betting on the dog. In the first place, he knew it was there. Then, Tim reasoned, a wild animal might have no taste for anything but fresh-killed meat. Lobo must surely have been accustomed to store food at one time, anyway. Tim jumped back down and got out the fresh tin he'd brought. The old pie plate was where he'd left it by the post. But it wasn't propped up any longer. Had Lobo come down and inspected it? Then perhaps Tim could put the food in the pan today, and leave it there on the ground? He decided against it, though. Better go slow, he cautioned himself. Maybe tomorrow, or the next day, he'd be safe in using the plate.

When he'd dumped the contents of the tin on the same ledge and got down again, he backed off and looked up at the rock. It was still bare as far as he could see. He walked on back to about the middle of the pasture. From here he could see most of the rock's flat top, and he sat down and prepared to wait.

Now and again he glanced back to where Cheyenne was grazing. He began to wish he'd brought something for himself to eat. But he'd been lucky to snatch the dog food, and he hadn't thought of anything else at the time. He looked back to the rock once more, and now his pulse gave an excited thump. Lobo had come out on the rock. He was out at the very edge, the way he'd been the first day. Tim raised his arm and waved. The dog didn't move. But he was looking straight at Tim, all right. Tim decided not to move any more himself. If he could just sit as quietly as Lobo was standing, and keep on looking back at him in a friendly, unthreatening way, it might do the trick. For a number of minutes he was able to be motionless. Surely the dog must be feeling safe. He might even begin to get curious. "All animals are nosy," he'd heard his father say. "Get 'em curious enough, and you've really got their attention."

The thing Tim hadn't counted on was that Lobo — or any animal, maybe — might be a lot more patient than he was himself. The minutes started to seem like hours, and he wanted to shift his position, at least. How could the dog just stand like that, without twitching a muscle, and without so much as blinking his eyes, apparently? There was a muscle jumping in Tim's arm where he leaned on it against the ground. His bent knee began to feel cramped. All at once he couldn't stand it any longer.

He sat up straight, put his fingers into the corners of his mouth and blew a strong, carrying whistle. He half expected Lobo to turn and trot off. Instead the dog cocked his head, the way he'd done the other time. Now, Tim told himself, if I can just make my voice carry. With both hands cupped around his mouth he shouted, "Lobo!" Truthfully, as he knew quite well, he was simply acting out of impatience. He admitted to himself later that the response he got was pure luck. He could take no credit at all for good timing, or anything else. But with his head still cocked in inquiry, Lobo waved his tail. It was a slow, tentative wave from one side to the other, and then down again. But it was enough for Tim! Of course the dog wasn't quite sure. He'd dropped his tail again quickly, and he'd given just one, uncertain wave. But it told Tim all he needed to know. It was so encouraging he felt

like leaping to his feet and shouting. He made himself get up slowly, instead. But then he couldn't resist starting to walk toward the rock, and moving a little faster than he should have. Lobo let him get about halfway there, and then he turned and trotted back out of sight. "Darn it!" Tim said. "You dope!" he told himself. He called himself a number of names. Lobo wouldn't appear again today, he felt sure, and he was disgusted with himself. But after a bit he shrugged almost cheerfully. It was real progress he'd made today, and this was no time to get discouraged. Starting back across the clearing he began to whistle a tune. Tomorrow, he thought, might be the day!

Riding back down the trail his mind was busy with speculation. Was it sheer chance that the dog had responded to the name "Lobo"? Would he have reacted to any call? Why had Aunt Kate used the name Lobo, anyway? He'd never thought to ask her if she'd heard the name of the mountaineer's dog. Maybe it had stuck in her mind without her exactly remembering it? She'd said that Lobo meant wolf. Still, Tim was wondering now. He was shy about asking her, though. It was all very well, he thought, for her to talk about getting another dog. He'd always known she'd never do it until old Mac went. But now he was wondering whether she'd be able to do it at all. He meant *ever*. Anyway, now was too soon. If he started talking about Lobo now she'd think he'd forgotten old Mac already. He was pretty sure about that. It would make her feel bad, and it might even prejudice her against Lobo. So how long might he have to wait even to bring up the subject? And then, what was the best way to go about it?

As *his* dog, she might accept Lobo. But then he began to think about going back home at the end of the summer. Tim's parents lived in the city and his father felt very strongly about big dogs in the city. It wasn't fair to them, he kept saying. "But some day we'll move out into the country," he'd often said, "and then you can have whatever you want." Tim had usually gone off grumbling to himself, "When I'm about a hundred years old, I suppose!" He wanted a dog now. He'd always wanted a dog now, about as long as he could remember. And for the first time in his life a dog was within his reach. A great dog! The greatest dog he'd ever heard of, actually.

Where the trail opened to the view of the ranch below, he pulled up Cheyenne. The horse knew that he was coming in to the home stretch. He'd begun to prick up his ears a short way back, and now he'd picked up his feet, too. Tim knew that any horse would break into a run, if you let him, when he got within smelling distance of home and the barn. Just try to get them out of the stable yard in the first place! Just try to keep 'em going down the road at a decent clip. But turn around and head for home and the tiredest acting old plug was suddenly as fresh and frisky as a colt. Tim shortened the reins further. "Stand, fella!" he said.

He scanned the corral and decided that Aunt Kate was probably home. He started going over in his mind what he might say to her. "Aunt Kate," he might begin, "you remember telling me about that mountaineer with the dog?" — No! That wouldn't do at all. He checked himself and started over again. "You remember telling me about that mountaineer? The one who got lost in the avalanche? Do you happen to remember the man's name?" That was it! She'd never catch on, from that, what he was really interested in. "Boy!" he said with satisfaction. And now he slackened Cheyenne's reins and let the horse take his head.

Coming down into the meadow he could see that there were three horses, reins down on the ground, grazing around the kitchen door. He recognized Shep's big bay mare. But he'd never seen the two pintos before. They were a nice pair, too. They were almost identical, and they weren't much bigger than Aunt Kate's pinto. Small, wiry, they looked like real cow ponies, the kind that could turn on a dime.

Tim's taste ran to bigger horses, long-legged and racy. But he'd gained a considerable respect for the tough little cow-pony breed. With any training at all they could run circles around an eastern type saddle horse in performance. For a roundup horse you couldn't beat them. He'd watched Buck or Trip throw a lasso, and seen the pinto brake to a stop, and then plant his feet and pull back to tighten the rope. The horse knew exactly what he was doing, and he was at least as important as the rider when it came to roping a calf. He'd stand there without moving until the calf was thrown and tied up. You had to respect that, he told himself. You even had to admire it. The rodeo slipped back into his mind. He'd see some great roping there, as well as some first-class riding. His father had taken him to the indoor rodeos back east. They were great and Tim had always enjoyed them. But this would be the real thing!

He curbed his curiosity about the strange horses, and rode Cheyenne around to the barn. When he'd ladled out some grain for the horse, he stopped to splash water from the trough onto his sweaty face and head. He'd got a really short brush cut before he left home and his hair hadn't grown enough yet to need a comb. His face was pretty tanned already.

He guessed he looked O.K., but he waited for the water's surface to clear. When it was still as a mirror, he looked down at his own reflection. He'd got the collar of his shirt kind of wet, but that would dry while he walked to the house. That was one of the advantages of this high, dry air. Aunt Kate could hang out a washing and have it bone dry in half an hour. His sandy hair had bleached almost white. His face was a lot darker than his head. He decided he looked pretty good, and set forth to meet the callers.

6

Shep was sitting at one side of the long trestle table, back to the windows, with a boy on one side of him and a girl on the other. Aunt Kate was across from them where she could get up easily and check on whatever was cooking. "Howdy, Tim," Shep said. "Thought we'd stop by and talk rodeo. My boy Danny here's on the parade committee." Danny stood up and put out his hand across the table. "Glad to know you, Tim," he said. His hand was hard and calloused. Tim said, "Same here." Danny wasn't quite as tall as Tim but he was every bit as rugged, and Tim guessed he was older. Fourteen — maybe fifteen? His sister was younger. She was about Tim's age, he thought. She might be a little less. When he glanced at her she smiled and Tim said, "Hi." She smiled like her father. Tim thought Shep always looked kind of sleepy, and very good-natured. He talked that way, too, very slow and with a drawl. Now he said, "Judy and Dan'll head up the cavalcade, and if you're riding Kate's pinto, you-all could make a nice threesome."

Tim looked at Danny who promptly said, "My idea." The questions in Tim's mind must have shown in his face: Was Shep just being nice? How did the kids feel about including him? "Thanks," he told Danny, while it went through his mind to wonder, now, if Aunt Kate had told them about his mother and they were being especially nice because they felt sorry for him. It didn't improve his confidence, and he felt as if he had to say, "But I'm kind of a greenhorn, you know." Aunt Kate said quickly, "You're all right! 'Course Tim's an Easterner," she told them, "but he's picked up a lot already. Learns fast." Tim shifted his feet. He was surprised, and he was pleased. But it kind of embarrassed him, at the same time, and he wished he could think of some way to get the conversation off himself. Then Judy said, "You can ride between us — me and Danny." She certainly had a nice smile, Tim thought again. But her brother seemed to be able to resist it. "Nothing doing," he told her firmly. "You got to be in the middle — it balances better that way. Me on one side, and Tim on the other. Heck!" he protested, "who got tossed just yesterday? We'll prob'ly end up taking care of *you*." Shep put back his head and laughed so heartily that the others

73

had to laugh with him. "Never did see a more surprised girl," he said then. "Wish I had a picture of your face, Judy." Judy looked a little self-conscious, but she took it like a good sport and didn't try to defend herself.

"Now then," Shep said, "why don't you kids make your plans while I talk to Kate?"

"I'm not trading Juanita," Aunt Kate said at once, "if that's still on your mind."

"Not for two colts?" he asked her, but Tim thought he was kidding, from his grin. "Matter of fact," Shep went on to say, "it's about your ranch." Danny and Judy had got up and come around to Tim's side of the table. But Tim wanted to listen to what Shep had to say about the ranch. "Got a buyer, if you're interested," Shep told her. Now Judy was listening, too. "Shep Hooston," Aunt Kate said, "you know right well I'm not selling my ranch to anyone but a rancher. If you've run into some more of those city folks want to turn the land into a playground, you can save your breath."

Tim had never thought of Aunt Kate giving up the ranch. Now he realized that the idea came as a shock to him. He wanted to speak out. He wanted to protest. But actually it was none of his business.

And then Judy spoke up again. "Oh, Miss Kate!" she said, "you can't give up the ranch! Where would you go? And what would we do if you weren't right here down the road?" That was kind of funny, Tim thought briefly. It was at least five miles to Shep's ranch. Still, there weren't any closer neighbors.

Aunt Kate spoke straight back to Judy. "I can and I will if I have to," she said. "I'm over seventy, and some days I feel it. But I'm danged and I'm hanged if I'll sell it for a playground."

They were all involved in the discussion now, and they all turned to Shep when he cleared his throat and prepared to answer her. "We gotta move with the times," he said. "Only offers you've got — only offers you're *apt* to get — come from the developers. Now there's talk of turning this whole area into a big resort. It's great skiing country — we all know that. Might bring the town back to life. Sure would bring in spending money."

"Spending!" Aunt Kate said fiercely. "That's all they think about. Who's going to feed the country? That's been our business," she said, "and we've done it well. Raising cattle, shipping them out, feeding the rest of the country. That's *real!*" she said. "That's what the land is for." A flush had

come up into her face. Tim had never seen her like this before, and he told himself that this was what she really cared about.

"Do you have to sell the ranch?" he broke in to ask because he couldn't keep still any longer.

"I don't *have* to do anything," she told him. "Except die when my time comes, like everyone else. That's independence," she told him, "or as close to it as anyone comes."

Shep cleared his throat again. He was looking at Aunt Kate but he was talking to Tim, answering Tim's concern. "No call to worry about Kate," he said. "Some of the richest land in the country, this here, and Kate owns her share of it free and clear. But she don't want to go on working forever. She'd maybe like to pull up stakes and see some more of the world. If she wants to, she's sure earned it."

Aunt Kate nodded briefly. "But I'll be hog-tied," she said vehemently again, "if I'll give up the land to the idle. You got that straight in your head, Shep Hooston?"

"Now, Kate," he said in his slow, soothing voice, "you know I understand how you feel. And I sympathize! But we've got to be realistic. Times change, and conditions change. You know as well as I do the government —"

Aunt Kate interrupted him by hitting the table with her fist. "Don't you talk to me about subsidies!" she told him angrily. Tim couldn't exactly follow the conversation now. But looking at Aunt Kate, and then looking at Shep's patient face he guessed maybe Shep might have the better of the argument. He guessed Aunt Kate half knew it, too, and that's why she had to be angry. It made him feel sort of bad, and when Aunt Kate suddenly turned and appealed to Dan and Judy, Tim was sure he was right. "You youngsters mind what I say," she told them. "The land is not for play!" A swift intuition swept Tim's mind. It wasn't really an idea Aunt Kate was talking about so much as a feeling. She was talking about what she loved. Shep was talking about facts, and she was talking about feelings. Tim remembered an old song his mother sang about "work is but grown-up play." He'd never really thought about the words. He'd always just liked the tune, and his mother's voice singing it. But now he was hearing the words, and understanding them. He guessed Aunt Kate didn't know it, but she *loved* to ranch, and raise cattle, and she couldn't stand anyone suggesting that maybe it wasn't every bit as important to the country as it always had been to her.

"Still — " Shep was saying, "we rent out horses to the dudes and mountaineers — "

"But it's not my business," she said sharply, "and I don't aim to make it so. The few stragglers who come through here don't crowd my cattle any."

Shep's gentle smile spread to a real grin. "Those reporters kind of crowded us all, though," he said. "Never will forget that swarm."

"When was that?" Tim asked him in a sudden alerted curiosity.

" 'Bout four years back," Shep replied. "Wasn't it?" To Tim's surprise it was Danny who answered him. "Four years last April," he said. "I was out of school with the mumps. I felt O.K. but I couldn't go to school so I tagged around after the newspaper men."

"That's when Danny decided he wanted to be a reporter," Judy put in.

"O.K.!" her brother said a little defensively. "But they were a darned nice bunch. They didn't treat me like a little old nuisance — which I prob'ly was."

Tim had turned to Aunt Kate and now he said, "Was that when the man got lost in the avalanche?" She nodded. "Came from Chicago," she said. "Or maybe it was New York. I don't rightly recall. But the reporters came from all over."

"Took some real good pictures, anyway," Shep said comfortably. He turned to Tim. "Even flew over in a plane," he said. "Guess Kate could use those aerial views for a survey map."

"Have you still got any of those pictures?" Tim asked Aunt Kate.

"Hmm — " she considered. "You might find some in the bottom drawer of my desk. Unlocked side."

Tim got out of the kitchen fast. Maybe, he was thinking, he might learn something about the dog. If Aunt Kate had kept some of the clippings along with the pictures, he might get some information about the mountaineer's dog. It was an off-chance, but it was the closest he'd come to running down anything at all.

Aunt Kate's "study" was an alcove off the sitting room mostly filled by a big old roll-top desk. Sure enough, the unlocked bottom drawer was crammed with papers, with maps and blue prints, and aged, yellowing newspaper clippings. The latter looked to Tim a lot more than four years old, but he guessed maybe newspaper discolored fast. He shuffled through and got a handful that seemed to carry photographs of the ranch. Back in the kitchen he made himself put them down, politely, in front of

Aunt Kate at the table. But then he couldn't resist picking out a few to go through himself. Danny moved over beside him, and together they began to pore over the clippings.

"Ever hear the definition of a mountaineer?" Shep asked idly to anyone who cared to listen. "Feller with a strong back and a weak head," he answered himself. Judy laughed, and Aunt Kate said, "Good description of that feller, all right. Never saw anyone so pig-headed in my life."

"Looked it, too," Shep said. "Kind of a wall around him. I remember I thought first he was blind —"

"You met him, too?" Tim looked up to ask.

"Sure did," Shep told him. "Right here in this kitchen. Him and that dog. One reason I thought he was blind," he explained, "him and that dog was touchin'-close the whole time. If the feller got up, the dog got up. When the feller sat down, the dog sat right down beside him. Had some crazy name — Tramp, or somethin' like that. Nice, pure-bred dog, from the look of him. You'd think he could have given him a decent name." Shep scratched his head. "Tramp — or Bum — or something real dignified like that," he said sarcastically.

"Hobo!" Judy said suddenly. "I remember now,

his name was Hobo. I thought it was cute." Tim suddenly relaxed all over, and now he realized how tense he'd been, trying to find what he was looking for in the clippings and listening to the conversation around the table at the same time. The tension went out of him so completely that for a second he felt limp. He dropped the clippings onto the table. He'd learned what he wanted to know, and it was all he could do not to speak about it. What luck! he kept thinking. No wonder the dog had responded to the name Lobo. It was almost the same sound. Lobo was a lot better, though. It was a great name for a great dog, and now, Tim told himself, it was going to be his name for good.

"You expected home for lunch?" Aunt Kate asked Shep presently. He brought his tilted chair back down onto the floor with a rap. "Sure are," he told her. "Is it late as that?" He stood up. "You kids got your plans worked out?" he asked them. Tim brought his mind back with a wrench from his thoughts of Lobo. There was something he'd meant to ask about the rodeo. Now what was it? Shep was clumping across the floor in his high-heeled cowboy boots, and now it came to Tim what it was he wanted to know. He turned to Danny. "Are we supposed to wear something in particular?" he asked

him. Danny glanced down at Tim's sneakers. "Well
—" he said, "you got any boots? Sneakers take a
good grip on the stirrup," he added quickly, "but
mostly we all wear boots." Shep turned around and
took a look at Tim's feet. "Guess I can rustle you up
an old pair of mine," he said. "Looks like your feet
are too big for anything of Dan's." Tim thanked
him. He was looking at Dan's and Judy's clothes.
They were dressed alike, in dungarees and faded-
blue work shirts. Judy had a red bandanna tied
around her neck, and Dan's bandanna was hanging
out of his hip pocket. "Are we supposed to all look
the same?" he asked Danny. "I mean — if we're
riding together, and out front —" He thought
Danny looked relieved. "That'd be a good idea," he
said. "'Course," he added, "everyone wears hats,
too. You know — ten-gallons? Mine's black. Judy
has a tan one." Tim nodded. "So I better wear a
black one," he said.

"Guess we can manage that," Aunt Kate put in.
Then she smiled, one of her rare, brief smiles of
amusement. "Thing to do," she said, "is get the
widest brim you can find and then roll it up narrow."
Shep laughed his deep, contented laugh. "You don't
miss a thing, Kate!" he told her. "Come on now,
kids."

Tim followed them outside and stood around while they got onto their horses. He had the need to say again, "I sure hope I can do O.K." It would be so awful, he kept thinking, if he didn't do them credit. At that Aunt Kate, from the kitchen door behind him, said, "Pshaw! Nothin' to it. Just ridin' around the ring."

Shep had swung into his saddle. "Nicest part of the whole show, though," he told Tim. "The rest's all competition. Only the parade's pure cooperation. That's nice," he said comfortably, just before heading his horse toward the road. Judy was right behind him, and Dan was bringing up the rear. "We'll stop by again," Dan said, "and go over the details. Or — tell you what — " he said, turning in his saddle to call back, "why don't you come over to our place? We're having a cookout Wednesday night. Why don't you ride over? About sundown. O.K.?"

"O.K.," Tim called after him. "Thanks." He wondered if he'd ever look the way they all did on a horse. He could sit a canter all right, he figured. But they were trotting, and not one of them moved in the saddle, not even Judy who was about half his size, and no more than twelve, he guessed now. Still — she'd got thrown. Maybe anyone could. It made him feel a little better, and he started back into the house thinking about the rodeo, and then the cookout. He'd have a lot to write his mother. And she'd be happy about it. All at once he could see her smiling. He could see her as clearly as — well, Judy, smiling at him five minutes ago.

7

EVERY day during the next week Tim found some time to get up to the high pasture. Now that he knew the dog's name he wasn't shy about calling him. First he'd whistle when he got to the clearing, and then he'd start across the pasture calling, "Lobo! Here, boy. Come on, Lobo!" The dog never failed to appear, and he never failed to respond in some way. He always cocked his head, and he usually waved his tail in a tentative, inquiring sort of way. But he never came down from the top of the rock. At least he hadn't yet come down while Tim was there.

All week Tim had been putting the food on the plate, down in the pasture, and he felt sure Lobo was getting it. At the end of the week he decided to make the experiment of hiding. He went back across the clearing into the trees as if he were leaving by the trail, as usual. He even called out a number of times, as he always did when he left: "I'll be back, Lobo! I'll be back." A short way down the trail he turned and started cautiously back, circling and keeping out of sight behind one tree after another. He crept the last short distance on his hands and knees. He was absolutely sure Lobo couldn't see him, and he'd already checked the wind and knew it couldn't carry his scent. Even so Lobo wasn't moving in any hurry. He'd even sat down, as if he had no intention of moving at all. Tim prepared to wait, and he fished out of his hip pocket his last letter from his mother. His father always wrote him once a week, but his mother generally wrote more often. Her letters were never very long. He supposed there wasn't much news if you were just in bed the whole time. Mostly she answered his letters and made comments on what he was doing. She always said how much she loved him, and how proud she was of all he was learning. It was a number of days now since he'd heard, and he really knew this letter by heart. Still he read it again. "I can hardly wait to hear more about Lobo!" she'd written. Well, he'd told her more by now, and he'd certainly like to get her next letter. Even air mail, he thought, was pretty slow. Meantime it made him feel good every time he read about Lobo. She really wanted Tim to win the dog's friendship. That was clear. "If you can just be patient —"

Well, he didn't need to read that part again. She'd always talked to him about patience and how it was something everyone needed to learn. But now he was *being* patient, and he'd written and told her so. He'd sure like to get her answer, too. How many days was it — ?

He glanced up toward the rock again, and then he stuffed the letter back into his pocket. Lobo had started down the face of the rock. Tim watched his light, sure-footed progress from one ledge or crevice to another. Where the fence post met the rock, Lobo paused, gathered himself, and took the leap to the ground as gracefully as a deer. He was no old dog, that was obvious. He must have been really young — probably no more than two, Tim figured — when he'd lost his master. That would bring him to six now, a good age for a shepherd. He'd have plenty of strong years ahead of him. He carried no excess weight. As far as his health was concerned, his life in the open would have done him more good than harm. Tim bet he had the muscles that no house dog could ever have developed. He'd have the split-second timing of a wild creature, too. Still Tim wondered, as he watched Lobo gobble the food, how the dog was going to get back up the face of the rock again.

The answer seemed to be that he wasn't. When he'd finished the food, he turned and trotted straight across the pasture toward the brook at the far side. Tim had to move in order to keep the dog in sight, and by the time he'd got to his knees, and then to his feet, the dog was nowhere to be seen. How do you like that? he asked himself. He decided that he liked it. In fact it made him smile with satisfaction. Sure, he thought, another trick of the wild. Always have an avenue of escape. Never get yourself into any place you couldn't get out of by another route, if need be. What a dog! he thought proudly. Just the same, he'd have to check that far side of the fence one of these days. If Lobo had a way through, so did the wildcats. Whether it was through, or over, or under, it needed looking into.

Tim dusted the pine needles and leaf mold from his pants and started to call automatically, the way he did every day, "See you tomorrow, boy!" But then he remembered that tomorrow was the day of the rodeo. He was meeting Dan and Judy in town at ten. That meant he'd need to start out about nine. He had all the usual chores to do first, and then harnessing for Aunt Kate. The horses would all need to be curried and groomed to perfection for their public appearance, especially Dexter and Sinister who would be up for judging. The palomino was being shown, too, but Tim guessed that Buck would take care of that. Still, any way he figured it, he couldn't see how he'd be able to get up to the high pasture in the morning. Maybe late in the day, when they'd all got back from the rodeo? He'd hate to miss a visit with Lobo. Maybe he could run up after supper, he told himself, and turned away reluctantly. He wished he had something special to leave for Lobo this time.

The next morning proved to be even busier than Tim had expected. "I think we'd better put martingales on the team," Aunt Kate said at breakfast. "And on your pinto, too. Town's one thing, but town on rodeo day is something else again." Tim had seen the martingales hanging in the barn, but he'd never really examined them. "How do they go?" he asked now. "Well," Aunt Kate told him, "the idea's to prevent the horse from throwing back his head. There's the running martingale, and that divides like a Y. One end attaches to each rein. The standing martingale goes straight and hooks onto the chin strap of the bridle. They're both the same at the other end, and *that* end is fastened to the cinch. Cinch goes through it. You'll see the loop. You can put running martingales on the team," she said, "but I'd use a standing on the pinto." "Do you expect him to act up?" Tim asked. Aunt Kate simply quoted, " 'An ounce of prevention is worth a pound of cure.' I've seen a feller get his face smashed. Least you might get would be a broken nose. Ever have a horse's head hit you, you feel as if you've been hit with a sledge hammer. Solid bone, and hard as a rock."

So on top of saddle-soaping all the rest of the leathers and polishing all their metal, Tim had to do the martingales as well. By nine o'clock he felt as if he'd done at least a half day's work. When Buck backed his pickup truck into the yard and said, "You want a hitch to town?" Tim had a weak moment of temptation. Back home he was used to being driven most places he went, or else hopping a bus or a subway train. That had nothing to do with being tired, either. He'd never worked hard enough to feel the least bit tired, up to now.

Buck ran up his truck to where he could most easily attach the horse trailer. He was taking the palomino who was to be shown "in hand." Tim understood that meant like walking a dog on a very long lead. It was only done with stallions who couldn't be safely ridden. But Buck could just as well hitch on the double trailer and take the pinto along too. Tim looked a little wistfully at the truck's comfortable, broad front seat. He could be driven to town, and back again, and save his strength for performing when he got there. But just at that moment Aunt Kate came out, all ready to drive off. She looked so tiny, and determined, and — sort of spunky — that Tim said, "No, thanks." If Aunt Kate wasn't letting herself be transported, why should he? He was thinking of Dan and Judy, too. They'd have set out already, and they had five miles farther to go than he did. Dan had explained that they'd stop by for him except that, being in charge of the parade, Dan had to get there early and get the other kids lined up. "Suit yourself," Buck answered him. "I'm entirely accustomed to being the only motorized critter in this outfit." He was a short, bow-legged man with a slight limp. He claimed his legs had been as straight as anyone could want until they'd got "saddle-sprung." His limp was the result of a bad fall from a bronco he was trying to bust. No one could take him for anything but a horseman, and right now he was dressed like a rodeo performer on the national circuit. His hat was pure white. His shirt was cream-colored, and pure silk. His light beige pants were brand-new, and so were his boots. It was he who would be showing the palomino, and that was what he was dressed for. He practically matched the big golden horse with the spectacular white mane and tail. It gave Tim, in fact, a moment's doubt about his own appearance. But Danny had helped him with it and Danny thought it was all right. He'd explained to Tim that it was usually the older fellows or the professionals who went in for the fancy duds.

By the time Tim got to town he was thirsty and he was beginning to be hungry and the last thing on his mind was how he looked. Still he noticed that Dan was right. All the young fellows he saw were wearing black hats, dungarees, and pretty plain dark shirts. It was almost a uniform, and thanks to Dan's advice he conformed. He headed for the hitching rail back of the post office where they'd agreed to meet. The matched pintos were there already and Tim rode in close beside them to tie up. Dan and Judy would be around at the front, on the steps, but Tim went through the back door in order to check on the mail. There just might be a letter from his mother. Aunt Kate's box was empty. But perhaps the mail wasn't all sorted yet?

So he went to the window and asked, too. "Miss Kate got ahead of you," the man told him. "Nothin' more now till noon."

Dan had said, "The town'll be hopping," and it was. Tim hadn't seen so many people since he left the city. He'd never, anywhere, seen a crowd quite like this one. There were farmers' wives in cotton aprons and women in spangles looking like circus riders. There were summer people from the hotels and dude ranches wearing city clothes, and there were grizzled old characters in rags who looked as if they'd come up off the desert, or down out of the mountains where they'd been prospecting without luck all their lives. There were "pros" in embroidered silk shirts and tooled-leather belts and boots. There were balloon men and popcorn vendors. Hot dogs were being roasted on outdoor grills. A clown was riding a donkey too small for him down one side of the street, while up the other side came three cowboys in an ancient car that had been rigged to "buck." Across from the post office a tall Texas cowboy leaned against a deserted store front playing his guitar and singing a song about the streets of Laredo.

Judy spotted Tim first and called out to him. A minute later Dan finished his conversation with some boys and girls who were going to be in the parade, and turned to greet Tim. To Tim's relief he said at once, "I'm starved. Let's get some food. We've got about twenty minutes." Judy agreed to stay and answer questions, and they agreed to bring her back a hot dog.

"Say!" Danny began when they'd crossed the street. "Will you do me a favor?" Tim said, "Sure!" without hesitating. "Thing is — " Dan told him, "I'm going to try out for one of the purses. But I don't want Judy to catch on. So if you'd kind of — distract her, while I slip away. O.K.?" This time Tim said, "Well — sure — " with a lot less conviction. "But what am I supposed to *do*?" he asked anxiously. "Oh," Dan assured him, "You'll think of something. Take her to get some pop. Or go look for Miss Kate. You know! I'll give you a sign when the time comes."

Tim thought of a number of questions. But really, he told himself, it was none of his business. Besides, he was pretty sure he knew what Danny was up to — he was planning to ride one of the broncs. Tim could have sworn to it. It was dangerous, and any kid who had the nerve to try it was bound to want to conceal it from his family. Tim tried to keep his thoughts to himself, but finally he blurted out, "Does

96

Shep know what you're doing?" Danny laughed. "No," he said truthfully. "And he'd prob'ly want to skin me alive. But he had a go at it too, when he was my age." He shrugged so cheerfully that Tim's worry gave way to a brief, secret envy. "I stand to make fifty bucks," Dan finished. Or to break your neck, Tim thought, and now his worry was coming back in full force.

In one way, though, Tim decided, it was a good thing to have something on his mind besides himself. As they set off, three abreast, for the rodeo field, he was giving a minimum of attention to his riding, and it had never gone better. He was even able to keep his horse in step with the others. The field was about half a mile beyond the far end of town and when they got in sight of it, Tim could see that the bleachers were crowded with people, flags were flying and a band was playing.

It was a pretty sight, the green field rimmed with blue hills, and then the grandstand alive with all the movement and color of hundreds of people. But his eyes swept the grandstand briefly and went straight to the center of the field where the chutes were set up, with the judging tower above them. From one of those wooden chutes Danny would come streaking out on a horse that was determined to throw him. If the horse won, Danny could be killed, or he could be crippled for life. What should Tim have said to him? And was there anything he could do to stop him now? Danny was his friend. But he was fifteen. He belonged here. He'd grown up with horses, and on them. What influence could Tim possibly have? His thoughts went around and around and arrived at no solution.

When the parade had circled the field and passed the grandstand twice, the riders disbanded and Tim followed Dan and Judy who cantered off around the end of the bleachers. They tied up their horses to the struts of the bleachers and started back to where, Dan assured them, seats were being saved for them. The loudspeaker at the judging tower was being tested. A roar was followed by a whisper and the crowd broke into laughter. A rancher who was a friend of Shep's had saved space for them on a front-row bench. Danny had lost his program, but he seemed to know it all by heart. He called the Roman races, and then the flat races, before the loudspeaker announced them. He was hunched forward and apparently giving his undivided attention to the track. But Tim thought he was keyed up, and Tim knew why.

When two or three events had been run off, the

clown came out on the field riding his under-sized donkey. It was the signal for a change of pace, and Tim saw Danny tense, and then fix his attention on the chutes. After a minute he felt Dan's elbow in his ribs. "UH — " Tim exploded as if the sound had been pushed out of him. He felt as if he'd give anything to just keep still, to ignore the whole thing and let Danny hang from the horns of his own dilemma. But he'd agreed to this. He was stuck with it. "I wonder where Aunt Kate's sitting?" he said. Dan picked it up like a flash. "Why don't you go look? Good time, right now. You won't be missing anything. Bring me back some pop, will you, Judy?" he added. Judy looked a little surprised, but Tim quickly said, "Come on, Judy. Where'll we start looking?" He was so nervous he expected his teeth to chatter, or his voice to break. He heard Judy's voice but he didn't take in half she was saying. Afterward all he could remember was that they never did find Aunt Kate, but they found the pop man, and a fellow selling cotton candy.

Before they got back to their bench the loud-speaker was announcing some bronc riding. "Now where's Danny?" Judy complained as they climbed over the rail that separated the bleachers from the track. "He'll just plain *die* if he misses the bronc

riding. That's his favorite part of the whole show."
It was all Tim could do not to voice his gloomy
thought that Danny might die if he *didn't* miss it.
The voice from the speaker spared him the need to
say anything. "Out of chute number three —" The
voice faded and died. Tim and Judy both looked
toward the chutes. Some rearing, rampaging horse
was thrashing around in number three. They could
see his plunging head, and they could even *hear*
him, thudding against the wooden sides of the chute.
The announcer's voice rang out again, "Out of chute
— " Tim had a crazy impulse to cover his ears. But
what good would that do? He tried to cross all his
fingers at once while he hoped — while he *prayed*
— it wasn't Danny.

"Out of chute number three — and this time he's
really comin' — Danny Hooston on Dynamite."
With that the door to the chute was opened and
held, and the biggest, blackest, twistingest horse
Tim had ever seen catapulted onto the field. He
seemed to be going in at least three directions at
once: sidewise, and up and down and forward. He
twisted, and bucked and zigzagged, and still he
seemed to be going down the field as if he'd been
shot out of a gun.

By now half the crowd was standing, and most

of them were whistling or shouting. Tim almost wished that Danny would be thrown at once and get it over with. Close to him a cowboy with a Texas drawl was saying, "That ain't no horse. That's a buckin' rattlesnake." Judy had grabbed his arm in both her hands and was hanging on. "Oh, Tim," she kept saying, "it's Danny. He'll be killed! Oh, Tim, he'll be killed." It was exactly what Tim expected, but somehow to his own surprise he heard himself saying, "He's still with it." A second later the whistle blew.

When they'd watched Danny jump clear, do a couple of somersaults and come up on his feet, they both sat down as abruptly as though the bench had reached up and snatched them. Tim said, "Whew!" and Judy let out a long, shaky breath. "He'll catch it when he gets home," she said then. "But — " She turned to Tim now and her eyes were shining. "He was great, wasn't he?" Now Tim was really envious. Now that the strain was over he felt pretty annoyed with Danny who had got him all upset for nothing. He'd certainly like to have the fifty dollars himself. And he'd like to have Judy admiring him, too. All in all he couldn't resist saying, "He was darned lucky. He could have broken his neck." Judy groaned. "Don't let's even *think* about it," she

said. "Oh, Tim, I'd have just *fainted* if it hadn't been for you. You were so *calm*." Tim started to say dumbly, "I was?" but he stopped himself just in time. It was beginning to occur to him that Judy had a pretty high opinion of him, and maybe the less he said, the better. "I don't know how you could be so calm," she said again. "I was a wreck!" He settled for saying, "Girls are different."

The loudspeaker had announced another bronc rider. "Meanwhile," the voice continued, "the teams will be gathering at the west end of the field — " Judy said, "Now we'll see Miss Kate! Oh, I hope she wins! Danny says the entries are bigger this year, in every class." Tim hadn't given much thought to Aunt Kate's part in the show. But now that it was almost upon him, and Judy was being so thrilled about it, he began to feel anxious. It was being a heck of a day! he thought suddenly. He'd expected it to be great. He'd really looked forward to it. And here it was just one strain after another. Now he'd have to worry about someone beating out Aunt Kate. Shep was right, he told himself, and things were too competitive. Cooperation was much nicer.

But when the teams finally started moving down the track a great pride rose up in Tim's heart because Aunt Kate was in the lead. It was the first time he'd ever seen her without her shawl. Her short, white hair was uncovered, and from the leather strap around her neck an outsized Stetson swung jauntily at her shoulders. The hat served to conceal her hump as effectively as the shawl, and it had a lot more style. Tim was impressed.

Judy had stood up and was scanning the line of teams with a practiced eye. "Danny's right," she announced. "There's real competition. But Miss Kate's got the best team," she maintained. "And no one can drive better than she can." As the teams came abreast of the grandstand, and passed, Tim did his best to study them as knowingly as Judy was doing. There was only one thing he was sure of, though: everyone appeared to be driving except Aunt Kate. She wasn't fussing with the reins, or speaking to the horses, or doing anything at all. The way she looked, she might have been sitting in a chair with her hands in her lap. Yet none of the other pairs was going with the precision and the grace of hers. Tim turned to Judy. "Are they clapping for Aunt Kate?" he asked her. Judy nodded. "Everyone knows Miss Kate," she told him. "And everyone loves her." Tim remembered thinking that Aunt Kate was a funny sort of person to feel fond of. But that was a long time ago! "She'll win," Judy said with confidence. "Because everyone wants her to — and because she's the best, of course."

When the judging was over and Dexter and Sinister were wearing blue rosettes on their bridles, Aunt Kate was asked to drive past the grandstand once more, by herself. Tim's throat was tight, and he wouldn't have trusted himself to speak. He thought of his mother, and he felt as if he could hardly wait to write it all to her. It was a few days since he'd written — and how long was it since he'd heard? He was afraid it was maybe as much as a week, and he generally heard every few days. If Aunt Kate didn't go in to town, Shep always did, and he always stopped by with their mail.

"What's the matter?" It was Judy, leaning toward him and looking into his face. She was looking concerned, as if he were — sick, or something. "Nothing," he said quickly. "I was — well, I was just thinking about my family, and all," he said. Now Judy smiled. "Are they all like Miss Kate — and you?" she asked him. It made him feel a little better. Still, he'd like to get hold of Aunt Kate right now and see if there'd been a letter for him this morning. "Do you get homesick?" Judy asked him next. She wasn't looking worried now, but she wasn't smiling any more, either. "I expect I would," she said. "I've never been away from home." So now he was able to admit it. "It's worse than you think," he told her. "I mean — I didn't want to come in the first place." Maybe he ought to apologize, or explain, or something, he thought briefly. Maybe he ought to say that it had nothing to do with this place, which was great, and everything. But somehow, with Judy, he didn't seem to have to explain. "I didn't want to *leave*," he said simply. Judy just nodded. "But my mother's sick — " he glanced at Judy again. "Maybe Aunt Kate told you she's in the hospital." He guessed he didn't really want to hear whether Judy had been told or not because he rushed right on. "And I figured — well, I'd like to *be* there. I don't know — " he said. "I mean there wouldn't be anything I could *do* — but — "

"I know what you mean," Judy said. "You do?" he asked her earnestly. If she really did, then he wished she would tell him, because he wasn't quite sure himself. "Well, if you were there," she said, "you could anyway *see* her every day." It was so exactly what he'd said to himself that he had to swallow before he could just say, "That's right. 'Course she *writes* me all the time," he added quickly, in case she should get the wrong idea. "But my father — " he began, and then he stopped. He hadn't exactly worked this out in his own mind, but his father had something to do with his feelings.

They'd both sat down, more or less simultaneously, and now he was dimly aware of the voices of the people around them. He wasn't really hearing them, though. After a bit Judy said, "You mean your father sent you out here?" That was it! Judy seemed to understand everything. "My mother misses me," he said. "I mean, I think she really misses me." Judy nodded solemnly. "Maybe she misses you even worse than you miss her," she said. At that Tim looked away. Maybe it was true. There was his mother just lying in bed the whole time with nothing to do, and nothing much to think about. And here he was — well, most of the time, anyway — busy, and getting acquainted with Lobo, and coming here to the rodeo, and getting to know Judy, and Dan. "Gosh!" he said fervently, "I never really thought of it that way." Judy suddenly smiled again. "Well, don't get all upset about it," she advised him. "I expect it's really much harder on you!

I mean, they're *together,* and all — "

"Hey!" Tim said. He didn't know why, but all at once he didn't want Judy to say any more. "Let's go find Aunt Kate," he said. "O.K.?" Judy agreed, "O K.! And we'll congratulate her!"

8

T<small>IM</small> and Judy finally found Aunt Kate back of the grandstand. The team was standing a few yards away, and Aunt Kate was surrounded by a little group of ranchers. None of the men was really tall, but they all loomed over her tiny figure. Tim gathered that they were all talking about the palomino. "That's the fee," Aunt Kate was saying in her direct, matter-of-fact way. "And you know there isn't his equal in the county. Only horse in the outfit I've got papers on." When she glanced in their direction, Judy went straight over, while Tim realized that even little Judy was bigger than Aunt Kate.

"Oh, Miss Kate!" Judy said, "we're so pleased!" Then, to Tim's amazement, she threw her arms around Aunt Kate and hugged her. Aunt Kate sort of grunted. "Speak to the horses," she said. "Credit's all theirs." But Tim saw that she shot a look at him. It came to him that she was a lot more pleased than she'd ever let on, and that she wanted him to be pleased, too. It made him feel shy, and his mind fumbled for the right thing to say. Then Judy did it for him. "Tim's just popping with pride," she said. He was so relieved and so grateful that he felt like hugging Judy. And now he was able to say, "That's right!" He was rewarded by one of Aunt Kate's rare smiles. "Now then," she said in her customary, crisp way, "you want to hitch the pinto to the back of the buckboard, you can ride home with me." He did want to. At least part of him wanted to. It would be so nice and easy. And maybe Aunt Kate wanted his company. And then he'd be able to ask her if she'd got any letters at the P.O. But there was Judy — and where was Dan? He turned to her. "You riding back with Danny?" he asked her. For a second she looked uncertain. Then she said firmly, "I'd rather go with you and Miss Kate — if there's room for me, I mean. I expect Danny's staying in town awhile — "

Aunt Kate broke in to say, "Spending his loot, no doubt. You come along with us, Judy. Leave a note on Danny's saddle. Go along now," she said then, "while I finish up my business." Before they could thank her she had turned back to the men and was saying, "I can remember when a palomino was unheard-of in this region. Nothing but buckskins. And some people hardly know the difference today. But the palomino's coming up — " Tim and Judy had moved out of hearing, toward the pintos. Tim was fishing for a pencil and wondering if he had a scrap of paper to write on. It was a couple of minutes before he realized that Judy was being unusually quiet. She generally talked quite a lot, and he liked that. It made him feel comfortable. "What're you thinking about?" he asked her now. "Danny," she said. "You mean you think we should wait for him, or something?" "Oh — no," she said. She sighed. "He'll prob'ly go to the dance," she said. "What dance?" Tim asked her. "Oh, there's always a dance," she told him. He made a guess at what it was that was troubling her. "Would *you* like to go to it?" he asked her. At once it occurred to him that she might think he was inviting her. It was an alarming idea. But she knew better. "Oh, no," she said. She sounded as startled as Tim was feeling. "It isn't for kids," she explained. "Well, then," he said reasonably, "Danny can't go, either." But Judy said, "Oh, yes he can." Tim wished she'd quit sounding so kind of gloomy. "He's got fifty dollars," Judy said. "And he rode that Dynamite." Tim was beginning to feel envious again, and annoyed at the same time. "Heck!" he said. "What's so great about that? It was crazy, if you ask me. He could have

111

broken his neck," he said again. Judy was standing still now, and she began to push around some dirt with the toe of her riding boot. "I don't know — " she said finally. "It's just — I mean, it's as if he's grown up, all of a sudden." She looked up at him. But she wasn't really seeing him, and he was shocked by how tragic she looked. "He didn't tell me about riding Dynamite," she said. "He didn't want me to know." She looked down at her feet again. "And he always told me things — and we always did things together. Now he'll never tell me anything again!" she said, and she sounded as if she were about to cry.

"Well, heck!" Tim said. "Gosh!" He was beginning to understand what she meant, but what could a person do with a thing like this? He had to do something, though. At least he had to say something. "Everybody has to grow up sometime," he said, "I guess." "But not *yet*," Judy said. It was sort of a wail. Any minute now she was going to burst into tears. He was sure of it, and it gave him a wild, helpless sort of feeling, as if something were bursting inside him. He wanted to throw his arms around her. But then he thought of something else, and that made him feel much better. "I'd like to punch him in the nose," he told her.

After a minute Judy laughed. It was a shaky sort of laugh, and when she looked up again, he saw that there were tears in her eyes. But she was laughing. And then she said, "Oh, Tim, you're so nice! You're the nicest boy I ever knew — except Danny!"

"Hmph!" Tim said. He could have said a lot more, and he'd have liked to. But he was so relieved to have Judy looking happier that he decided to keep still.

He'd unearthed an unused picture postcard from his pocket. "We can use this," he said. "Why don't you write it while I hitch the horses to the buckboard."

As he untied his horse, and Judy's, he realized that the sun was halfway down. It was shining straight into his eyes. He hadn't taken in the fact that it was so late. At this rate, it would be dusk before they got home. He wondered what they were having for supper. Maybe Aunt Kate would ask Judy to stay. If she didn't think of it, he might remind her. Then he would have to ride home with Judy afterwards. Or perhaps he could drive her home? A fascinating picture came into his mind of himself driving Judy in the pickup truck. He'd driven the truck around the place. He knew exactly how to handle it. Back home he'd have to have a license, of course, to drive without an adult in the car. He didn't know what the law was here, but he'd seen kids no older than himself driving around the town. He wondered if Buck would be back in time. Then he wondered what Aunt Kate would say. One thing he was sure of, though — Danny couldn't drive any better than he could!

It was a nice ride home. Aunt Kate was taking it easy because of the pintos trotting at the rear. The sun was going down fast now, and a coolness was coming into the air. It seemed to come up from the

fields beside the road like a mist, and it smelled of sweet hay, and sagebrush. Judy was talking again in her usual lively way, and she got Aunt Kate to talking, too, going over the rodeo, and reminiscing about earlier days. Tim felt peaceful and good just listening to them, and smelling the sweet air and thinking about how he just might get to drive Judy home in the pickup truck. A single, brilliant star came out in the deepening blue of the sky, and as they turned into the ranch road, Aunt Kate said, "Going to have a full moon tonight."

There was no sign of the truck or the horse trailer at the barn. Aunt Kate dropped the reins, got down, and said, "If you'll take care of the team I'll start supper." To Judy she said, "I'll phone your mother. Tell her you're eating with us." Judy thanked her, and Tim said, "Aunt Kate, do you think Buck'll be back from town?" "Doubt it," she told him. "If I know him, he'll stay till the last dog's hung." With that she left for the house.

Tim's dream began to fade. But in no time at all he'd started in on a new one. "You ever ride at night?" he asked Judy. "I mean — in the moonlight, and all?" She'd started sponging the leathers while Tim wiped the bits. "Oh, sure!" she said. "Sometimes we take a cookout up the mountain and ride back in the moonlight. I love it! 'Course," she added, "horses don't see too well at night so you just kind of poke along. You feel like galloping!" she said. "You feel like racing the clouds. It's nice, though," she said more quietly, "just poking along. Sometimes everybody sings." She paused and now a dreamy look came into her eyes. "Danny's got a wonderful voice," she said. "He could go on TV."

"You finished with that sponge?" Tim asked her. "I'm hungry!"

After a surprised second Judy laughed. "Come to think of it," she said, "I'm starved."

They always ate in the kitchen, but tonight Aunt Kate suggested that they use the sitting room and have a fire in the fireplace. She had a steak for them and Tim grilled it over the open fire. It was almost like a cookout, with Judy sitting on the floor and saying, "Nothing *ever* tasted so good!" The only difference, Tim thought drowsily after a bit, the air outdoors kept you awake. He was beginning to feel sleepy. He'd left the horses saddled, and now he told himself they'd better get started. He was just going to say so when his attention was caught by the sound of a car outside. "Hey!" he said, wide awake all at once, "Buck's back." Aunt Kate got up. "Expect it's Shep," she said. "Come to fetch Judy." Tim got to his feet a little clumsily, and when Judy put up her hand he gave her an absent-minded lift. "Heck!" he said. "I was going to ride you home." He felt disappointed, and he felt vaguely cheated.

It was Shep all right, with his truck and trailer, and Tim helped get Judy's horse into the trailer. Judy kept saying what a good time she'd had, but it was hard for Tim to say much of anything. At the

117

last minute Judy said, "It would have been a nice ride." She was looking at the moon, and for a minute Tim looked at it, too. It made him feel less bad. Still, when they'd left, and Aunt Kate had gone back into the house, he stood in the empty road without moving.

The moon was brilliant and seemed very close in the clear, high air. The sky seemed close, too, and the white scudding clouds made him think of what Judy had said about wanting to race the clouds. He felt restless — and something else that he couldn't quite give a name to. The air was sharp, and showed his breath like smoke. He shivered, but still he went on standing there. Maybe the word for what he felt was "lonely." Or maybe it was "scared." He began to think about outer space, and how it went on and on. But somewhere it must stop? He'd thought about this before, but not for a long time now. He remembered the first time he'd thought of it, and the weird, scared way it made him feel. He kept thinking there must be an end, even to the universe. But then what was beyond the end? It must have an end, because everything did. But how could it have an end? It was impossible to imagine, and trying to imagine it made him feel crazy, and terribly alone. He'd have to stop. He guessed what he was trying to think about was infinity, and he guessed maybe no one could really think about that. He thought about his mother. And now he wondered, again, why he hadn't heard. He'd meant to ask Aunt Kate, but he hadn't really had a chance. He'd go in and ask her right now. There might have been a letter today.

A cloud crossed the moon to darken the sky briefly. He watched for it to clear again, turning back toward the house as he did so. When the cloud passed he was facing up toward the trail where it opened to the broad view of the ranch. His heart thudded. Lobo had come out onto the overhanging cliff and stood there now, in the brilliant, white light, looking down at the ranch, and at himself. "Lobo!" he said, not softly, but not calling out, either. The dog waved his tail once. "You looking for me, Lobo?" he said then. It was the only time he'd ever seen the dog anywhere near the ranch. He'd never seen him at all except up in the high pasture. But this was the first day that Tim hadn't gone up looking for the dog. So Lobo must have missed him, and come down looking for him. It was the best sign Tim had ever had.

Tim had stopped shivering now. In fact he felt suddenly warm. It was like when he'd been swimming in a cold lake and all at once passed through a warm current in the water. "Come on down, boy!" he said. Or maybe he should go up? "Lobo!" he called again, with so much force this time that he almost shouted it. Now he was certain of the dog's interest. How could Lobo have given him a clearer sign? And once again the dog's loneliness seemed to fit right in with Tim's own.

The kitchen door opened abruptly and Aunt Kate's tiny figure was outlined against the light from within. "That you, Tim?" she asked. "Thought I heard someone call." With a sinking heart Tim saw Lobo turn and trot off up the trail out of sight.

What a mixed-up day, he was thinking, with so many nice things and so many awful things all one on top of the other. All at once the only thing he wanted to do was to get into bed and pull up the covers. First, though, he reminded himself wearily, he had to unsaddle his horse. He'd better hurry, too, he told himself next, because the light had just gone on in Aunt Kate's bedroom and he still hadn't asked her if there'd been a letter from his mother today.

9

Tim had gone to bed thinking about Aunt Kate's words: "No mail. Stopped twice, and asked at the window, too. Nothing but a couple of catalogues." Now he waked to start thinking about it again. This time he tried to really figure it back. It made him so nervous that he got up at once. It was a week — he was sure it was a week — since he'd heard from anyone. Oh, he'd had a post card from his friend Bart who had gone to some camp in Maine and wrote to tell him about catching a three-pound bass. Tim had gone camping with his father a summer ago and he'd caught a seventeen-inch trout. They didn't have anything to weigh it on, only a steel tape to measure it with. But Tim bet it weighed at least three pounds. He was pretty sure he'd told Bart about it at the time, though, so he probably couldn't remind him of it again now. Anyway, he had the rodeo to tell him about.

It really made him anxious to think how long it

was since he'd heard from his mother. He was washing and getting into his clothes in a hasty, clumsy sort of way. When he'd pulled a fresh T shirt over his head he heard the phone ring. A minute later Aunt Kate said, "Speaking." Then there was a silence before she said, "Yes," and again, "Yes." Tim paused at the head of the stairs. It didn't sound as if she were really talking to anyone, except the operator, and something about her voice kept him standing at the top of the stairs. After a longer silence she said, "Will you repeat that, please?" It must be the operator, he thought. Maybe it was a telegram? Well, that could be O.K. But Aunt Kate didn't sound as if it was. It made him curious, and it made him uneasy, and he waited until she'd said, "Thank you," and hung up, before going on down to the kitchen.

Aunt Kate was still standing by the phone, with her back toward him, and when he said, "Good morning," she didn't turn around. It was as if she hadn't heard him at all. When she finally moved, and then saw him, she said, "Oh, good morning, Tim," as if he'd surprised her by appearing without warning, and when she hadn't expected him. A second later she surprised him by suddenly sitting down on the nearest chair. "You all right, Aunt

Kate?" he asked her. He had to wait for her answer. "All right," she said then, but she said it sort of absently.

A terrible anxiety was growing inside him, and he finally had to say, "I heard the phone. Is — I mean — ?" He didn't know quite how to put it, and all at once Aunt Kate stood up. "I made oatmeal," she told him, "but maybe you'd rather have eggs." She went across to the stove with her quick, swinging stride. Now she seemed the same as ever. Still, he thought she wasn't, quite. "Oatmeal's O.K.," he said. "Aunt Kate? Is everything — all right?" He thought she started to say "all right" again, but then she stopped and really looked at him. "Your father's coming out," she said. "He just wired — " For a second Tim's heart lifted. "No kidding?" he said. "When?"

Aunt Kate had looked away from him again. You'd think she'd be as pleased as he was. You'd think — but he'd already begun to think beyond that. Why had she sounded so strange? And why was his father coming? How could he leave Tim's mother, alone in the hospital, and everything? The whole point, he told himself, the *whole point* was that he had had to stay, and Tim had had to leave. He seemed to be thinking slowly and very fast at the same time. "What did he say?" he asked now. "I mean, what did the wire say?" Aunt Kate brought two bowls of oatmeal to the table and set them down. "He's coming for a visit," she said. "He'll be here —" "But what about Mother?" Tim broke in. Now it was he who needed to sit down, and he pulled out a chair and dropped into it. "Is Mother all right?" he made himself ask. Aunt Kate pushed the cream pitcher toward him, and a dish of brown sugar with a spoon in it. He'd never had cream anywhere else like the fresh cream here at the ranch. It was thick, and almost yellow, and very sweet. It nearly made oatmeal taste like a treat. "Your father's coming out," Aunt Kate said again in a strange, stubborn sort of way as if it was something she'd memorized. "He'll tell you about your mother and —"

"Is that what he said?" Tim interrupted her. "He wants to tell me himself? Then —" He pushed back his chair abruptly, stumbled to his feet, and then turned his back. He heard Aunt Kate come up behind him and sort of hover there. She didn't touch him, though, and he was grateful for that. "Yes, Tim," she said, "he wanted to tell you himself. I'm sorry! — I meant to let him. I surely did. Tim!" she added then, "she was very sick. She couldn't —"

124

"O.K.," he said very fast in order to stop her voice from going on and telling him any more. He never cried in front of anyone, but the effort not to cry now was making a tight, hard pain in his chest and he could hardly get his breath around it.

Aunt Kate had begun to move now. She was walking up and down the room. "Go ahead and cry!" she said. "Or go out and cry, if you've got to. But you listen to me!" she said then, and she sounded almost angry. "Real men have got real feelings and it's no disgrace to them. You hear me?" Just before his shoulders began to shake he bolted out the kitchen door.

He had no idea where he was going, and even when he'd started walking he wasn't conscious of his direction. He just had to get somewhere by himself where no one could see him, and no one could hear him, and no one could speak to him. Something inside him kept saying, "No!" but the tears were streaming down his face by now, and he really knew it was true. He thought he should have stayed home. He thought someone ought to have told him — how sick his mother was, and what might happen. His father must have known. He'd even gone through medical school, and all. He must have known, and that was probably why he'd sent him away. It gave him a bad feeling, as if his father had betrayed him. Then he had a brief, bad feeling about his mother, too, as if she could have got well, as if she hadn't really tried. She was only — why, she wasn't *half* as old as Aunt Kate! But he told himself that was crazy, and he made himself think of something else. What was the matter with the doctor? That's what doctors were for, wasn't it, to make people well? Maybe it was a no-good hospital.

He was halfway up the meadow toward the trail before he stopped. Between the sobs that were shaking him, and the effort of climbing, he had to stop. After a minute he threw himself down on the ground and buried his face in the grass. There wasn't anyone to blame. That's what he'd been trying to do, as if that could make anything better, as if it could *change* it, really. Still — he wished his father had told him. He wished he'd stayed home. He wished — he wished — he pounded the hard ground with his fists in fury and frustration. The only thing he really wished was that it wasn't true.

After a while he sat up and rubbed his eyes hard with both hands. He needed a handkerchief badly and of course he didn't have one. What was it that Aunt Kate had said, anyway? He tried to go back over the whole thing. Maybe he'd misunderstood

126

her? Had she said — had she ever actually *said* — He shook his head. He knew better. Really, in a sort of way, he'd kind of half known from the first, when he'd heard her voice on the phone sounding so strange and not at all like herself. At least he'd known something was wrong. He guessed, remembering it now, that he hadn't exactly wanted to find out what it was. It would have to be something pretty bad to shake up Aunt Kate. He knew her well enough to know that.

The sun was hot on the back of his neck and along his arms, but a light wind was stirring. He looked up to the sky. There were little white, blowing clouds like puffs of smoke in the clear blue air. He thought of the sky last night with the moving, moon-lit clouds. What a long time ago that seemed now! Then he thought about Lobo coming out on the cliff above him, coming to look for him. That didn't seem so long ago. And all at once he knew where it was he wanted to go. He wanted to find Lobo. He had to find Lobo!

He looked back toward the ranch. There was no sign of life around the barns, and there was no smoke coming up from the bunkhouse chimney. Either Buck had slept over after his big night in town, or else he was off on his chores already. Tim figured he'd slip around to the back. He'd take one of the horses from the corral and not stop to bother with a saddle. When the horses were turned out, they all wore halters with a short rope attached that served well enough as a bridle. He'd seen some Indians at the rodeo yesterday riding with nothing but a halter and rope. And he doubted if even a cowboy rode any better than an Indian.

Once he'd got out of the corral and into the meadow, he headed the horse for the trail and kicked him into a canter. He knew the theory of sitting to a trot without the help of stirrups, but he hadn't mastered it. Bareback, he did a lot better at a canter or gallop. It was faster, too, and that suited him especially right now. He wanted to get away before Aunt Kate came out and saw him.

He wasn't noticing anything along the trail today. His mind was taken up with his goal. He wanted to get to the high pasture and find Lobo, and nothing could distract him but the memories that were mixed up with his feelings — his mother — Aunt Kate — old Mac — and then back to Lobo again. Now he was really understanding the strength of his feeling for the dog. Nothing that he could remember had ever struck so deep to his heart as the story of Lobo's loss. From the first time he'd heard the story he'd felt the dog's grief as keenly as if it were his own. And now he understood why. Now he could really admit how close it had come to himself, how exactly the dog's loss had resembled his own fears. It was sort of like, he told himself now, the fearful "warnings" of his dreams. Now he understood it all. And only Lobo, he told himself, could understand how he was feeling right now. The dog would come down to him today. He was absolutely sure of it!

For the first time Tim knew what Shep meant by a good walking horse. Shep always said a good walker was hard to find but there was nothing like it for a day in the saddle. Tim had always thought it sounded pretty dull, but now he was appreciating it. This horse was a good walker. He climbed the steep trail as smartly as though he were going along at a trot, and Tim was surprised how fast they got into sight of the pasture.

The minute he saw the clearing he looked toward the big rock. In the next minute all his attention was needed for the horse. The wide, free pasture, or perhaps the smell of the sweet mountain grass, put a sudden coltish spirit into the horse and he broke into a joyous gallop. Part way across the clearing he stopped abruptly and bucked. Luckily

Tim had taken a good grip with his legs when the horse started up, so he managed to stay on with the first buck. "Cut it out!" he told the horse, and gave him a slap with the halter rope. At that the horse skittered sidewise, and then bucked again. This time Tim sailed off. He was aware of holding fast to the halter rope, and he was aware of some out-cropping boulders around him in this part of the pasture. After that he wasn't conscious of anything.

When he came to his head was aching, but something warm and wet was going over his face. He opened his eyes and looked straight into Lobo's eyes. The dog was standing over him and licking his face. "Lobo!" he said. He started to put up his hand to touch him, but such a pain shot through his shoulder that he groaned, and lay still instead. Now the dog lay down beside him. "What happened, Lobo?" he asked after a minute. He was sprawled on his back, and the sun was very hot on his face. Maybe he'd been here quite a while? After a bit he realized that his head was resting against a rock. His position was very uncomfortable, but he felt even worse when he tried to move. He wondered where the horse was, but it was too painful to lift his head and look around. "I think I've broken something, Lobo," he said. He guessed he had broken his

130

shoulder. He'd probably landed on it, and then hit his head on the rock and blacked out. It must have happened all at once. He didn't remember landing at all. Lobo continued to lie quietly beside him, not offering to lick his face now, but looking at him in a companionable and protective sort of way.

Tim decided to try moving again. He figured he might move his legs without disturbing his shoulder. If he could get his knees up, and then sort of edge himself along with his feet, he might at least get his head off the rock. It didn't take him very long to discover that one of his legs hurt just as much as his shoulder. It was his left shoulder, and it was his left leg. Had he broken his leg, too? He lay motionless again and thought about it. If he couldn't walk, he was really in trouble. How could he possibly get down the trail again? He began to feel anxious, and a little scared. He was a long way from the ranch. No matter how loud he shouted, he could never make himself heard. He tried to remember whether Buck might have any reason for coming up to the pasture today. He doubted it. If Aunt Kate missed him, they might come looking for him. But that might take a good many hours of wondering and looking elsewhere. Perhaps he would be here all night? He'd brought nothing to eat or drink. He thought he'd heard or read somewhere that thirst could be more important than hunger, and that if a person just had some water to drink he could survive for quite a long time. He began to think about what it would be like to be out here, alone, all night. Would the wildcats come down? And what about the timber wolves? If a person was alive but helpless would a wild animal attack and kill him?

But Lobo would protect him! Lobo must have fought with wild animals before now. Lobo would fight off anything that attacked him. "You'd take care of me, wouldn't you, boy?" he said. The dog leaned over and licked his face again. Now he realized why it was that he wasn't more scared. He would have expected to be in a panic. And if it weren't for Lobo, he guessed he would be. He moved his good arm, carefully, and reached out to touch Lobo's head. His coat was thick and rather coarse, but his ears were as soft as flannel. They were as soft as the ears of a puppy, for all they stood up so strong and straight.

When Tim dropped his arm, Lobo dropped his head and rested it against Tim's hand. After a minute the dog sighed a deep, contented-sounding sigh. It was as if he had found his person again, as if he had come home. It was the way Tim had imagined it might be, and for a few minutes he felt so peaceful that he thought he might fall asleep. He could even think about his mother now in a quieter way. He remembered her coming to stand beside his bed when he was sick in the night, or when he'd waked up from a nightmare, maybe. But now he felt his eyes filling with tears again. He was wrong, and he couldn't think about her quietly. And he couldn't fall asleep either. And he'd have to do something. "Lobo," he said, "you'll have to help me." The dog lifted his head and looked at him. He put his head to one side, and then to the other. He was trying to understand what it was Tim was saying. "I've got to try to get up," Tim told him. Now the dog stood up, and looked at him even more questioningly.

Tim tried rolling himself gently onto his good, right side. It hurt, but it was possible. Now, he told himself, if he could just get up on one hand and one leg. The effort, and the pain, made him break out in a sweat, and a minute later he'd fallen back flat again. The pain that shot through him was so intense that for a second he thought he would faint. Lobo had backed off a bit and made a low, whining anxious sound. Now he came close again and began

134

to lick the sweat and the tears from Tim's face. "You've got to help me, boy!" Tim said again. Perhaps Lobo could drag him? Or perhaps he could go for help? He reached for the dog's mouth and tried to close it on his hand. If he could use his other hand, he thought he might manage it, and Lobo might get the idea. It was more than he could do, though, and the only idea Lobo got was to start licking his hand now. "That's all right, boy," he said. "Good boy." How could he tell him to go for help? He tried pointing back toward the trail. "Go, boy!" he said. "Go, Lobo!" Once again the dog put his head on one side, and then the other, inquiring, and trying to understand. "Go, Lobo!" Tim said again. "Go for help." The dog backed off a trifle, still searching Tim's face and looking uncertain. "That's right!" Tim told him. "Go!" And once again he pointed toward the trail. The dog backed off a little farther, but still without turning. Now it occurred to Tim that Lobo did understand, but that he was troubled and uncertain. He both wanted to go and he wanted to stay. He was afraid to leave Tim. That was it! And now Tim felt certain that he was used to obeying orders, and that he understood a great deal. He guessed he'd just have to be more firm. He'd have to insist. And then he had another idea. If he gave Lobo something to deliver — if he gave him something of his own to take it would be like a message to Aunt Kate, or Buck. If he had a belt, for example. But he wasn't wearing a belt. Even a handkerchief would do, he thought. "Darn!" he said, but — there must be *something* in one of his pockets!

The pain of moving was so intense that he nearly gave it up. But he made one last, desperate reach into his hip pocket. To his surprise he came up with a wadded handkerchief. It was a big, man's handkerchief, crumpled but clean. It was one of Aunt Kate's. She must have stuffed it into his pocket as he was leaving the house, and he hadn't even been aware of her touching him. He shook it out, and then reached to put it around Lobo's neck. Now he absolutely had to have two hands, in order to tie it. He gritted his teeth against the pain, and he broke out in a sweat. But he managed to tie the two ends loosely so that the handkerchief was secure around Lobo's neck. This was even better than something of his own, he thought. Lobo would get the message, as well as Aunt Kate. He'd get her scent, and go to her.

He was faint with the effort and the pain, but he had one more effort to make. He touched the handkerchief, and then he said, "Carry! Go!" When Lobo still hesitated, Tim hitched himself back up onto one elbow and pointed toward the trail. "Go!" he said again, and pointed so vigorously that it jolted his whole body. Now he felt dizzy, and a second later he had fallen back onto the ground, and everything went black once more.

10

WHEN Tim finally returned to consciousness it was like waking slowly from a long sleep, and he began to wonder where he was. He felt cramped and stiff. The next thing he realized was that he seemed to be enveloped in a curious odor. It was so strong that he suspected it had waked him up, as surely as a loud sound would have. But was that possible? Could a smell have that power? It wasn't an experience he'd ever had before, so far as he knew — unless, he reasoned, it was the smell of bacon cooking that waked him many mornings. This was a disagreeable smell. He turned his head in the effort to escape it. Now his shoulder stabbed him with pain again — and now everything was coming back to him. He remembered where he was, and all that had happened. He put out a hand to touch Lobo beside him. But Lobo wasn't there.

The disagreeable, pungent smell was very strong, and all at once he guessed what it was. It must be the smell Aunt Kate had told him about: wildcat!

She said he'd know it if he ever smelled it, although she couldn't exactly describe it. She'd said he was to look sharp if he ever caught that smell. But he couldn't move, except painfully to turn his head. Fear clutched him. Where was Lobo? And how could he have left him alone, at the mercy of any wild animal that might come down and attack him? But then he remembered that he had told the dog to go. He had ordered him to go, and fetch help. How long ago was that? The sun was no longer beating down on his face. He looked up at the sky. There were dark clouds overhead as if a storm were brewing. It was hard to tell just how late it was, but as nearly as he could judge, from a faint radiance behind the clouds, the sun had already crossed the midday sky. There was a fresh, cool edge to the air and the leaves of the aspens quivered in a rising wind. Tim thought of his mother and a forlorn and awful loneliness swept over him.

It was a number of minutes before he could think of anything else. Then he began to think about time again. He must have been here for a long time — and what could have happened to Lobo? He remembered Aunt Kate's handkerchief. But maybe he hadn't tied it well enough? Maybe Lobo had lost it — shaken it off, or caught it on a bush. He was still

conscious of the smell of wildcat, and now he
thought he heard a twig snap somewhere not far
behind him. Fear tingled his scalp and ran down
his spine like a shiver. Did he imagine it, or could
he hear padding feet that ever so slightly trembled
the ground beneath him? He wasn't imagining it.
He distinctly heard the light, sure-footed trot of an
approaching animal. In the next minute he saw
Lobo's head, and then the dog had dropped to the
ground beside him. Tim's relief was so great that
just at first he couldn't speak. When Lobo nuzzled
his head against him, Tim put out a weak hand and
touched him. He told himself that he ought to have
trusted the dog. He should have known that he'd be
back. Where had Lobo been, though, he wondered
next? Somewhere he'd lost the handkerchief; it was
no longer around his neck.

The dog had approached him coming from the
direction of the trail. So either he had been lying in
wait there, guarding Tim, and then maybe the smell
of wildcat had brought him closer, in protection?
Or else he had just come back up the trail. Maybe
he'd been up and down the trail more than once,
trying to find someone at the ranch, and then running back up to watch over Tim. Where was every-

one, Tim wondered? Where was Aunt Kate, or Buck?

Like an answer to his question he heard a shout from the trees over where the trail opened. It sounded like Shep's voice, and sure enough, when the two horses had cantered across the clearing and pulled up short beside him, it was Shep, and Danny with him. Lobo had lifted his head, and now he gave a low, warning growl. Tim tightened his hand on the dog's neck and said, "It's all right, boy!" It went through his mind that at least Lobo hadn't taken off at the sight of strangers. He must have settled his mind that he belonged with Tim.

Shep was sliding off his horse to the ground. "Tim!" he said, "you hurt bad?" Tim nodded. "I can't move very well," he said. "I guess I landed on my shoulder. But I did something to my leg, too. Left one." They were both looking down at him now. "What made you take that colt?" Danny asked him. "I could 'a told you — " Shep interrupted him. He was smiling his slow, sweet smile when he said, "I guess the colt told him." Tim looked back at Danny and said defensively, "He had the longest halter rope. I figured it gave me more to neck-rein with."

Shep had got down on one knee and begun to feel of Tim's shoulder. "How's your head feel?" he asked him then. "You sure picked a hard pillow." He put both hands to the back of Tim's neck and very gently tested its movement. "I blacked out," Tim told him. "When I came to my head ached — bad. But I think it's O.K. now. I blacked out twice," he added. "Did Lobo fetch you?"

Shep was feeling of Tim's hurt leg now, and it was Danny who said, "The dog came down, yeah. Where'd you pick him up, anyway?" he asked curiously. "Miss Kate thinks he's what she calls the ghost-dog. Says she never saw him down near the ranch before, though. He came right to the kitchen door."

Shep broke in to say, "That was the second time. First time, he just showed up on that outcropping — you know," he said to Tim, "where the trail starts, just above the ranch?" Tim started to tell them how he'd sent the dog, but Danny was saying, "First time, we'd just ridden into the yard. We didn't know what the dog was up to, standing there and baying at nothing, far as we could see. Miss Kate didn't know, either. So we just went in and visited a while."

"Don't know how long it was," Shep put in. "Then

the dog turned up at the kitchen door. When Kate went out, he took off. High-tailed it back up to the ridge. Then he turned and just stood there, lookin' back down at the ranch, and us. Tryin' to get someone to follow him is the way we finally figured it. Then Kate told us — " he paused and looked into Tim's face with a special, deep gentleness. "Tim," he said, "I'm downright sorry. I don't know how to tell you the way my heart goes out to you. Some time or another," he said, "we've all got to lose our mothers. It's the law of nature. But I don't guess it ever comes easy — and with you, it's just come way too soon." Tim felt the tears welling up in his eyes again. "You got to cry," Shep said, "you just go right ahead and cry. It's only natural."

All Tim wanted to do was to cry. But he looked at Danny. He was darned if he wanted to cry in front of Danny. "That's O.K.," he said, so fast that it came out like one word. "Thanks," he thought to add. "I guess — " he took a shaky breath. "I guess I've just got to get used to it," he managed to say. Then to his surprise Danny said, "I'm real sorry, too, Tim." He sounded as if he meant it. For the first time it occurred to Tim that Danny wasn't so very grown up, after all, and if his mother died, he'd cry, too. He might even bawl. "Thanks, Danny," he said. "Where's Judy?" he asked then. It was Shep who answered him. "Gone to some sewing bee at the 4–H Club. Now, Tim," he said firmly, "we got to figure out how to get you back down. Way I see it, we'll need a litter. Now I reckon I'll go back on down, get hold of a litter, call the doctor, and let Danny stay here with you." He glanced up at the sky. "That storm breaks," he said, "you're going to get real wet. Guess we better try to move him, Dan," he decided. "Get you over there under the trees you'll have a little protection, anyway." He dropped the cigarette he'd lighted and ground it into the earth with his foot. Then he directed Danny to take Tim's legs while he very gently got Tim's shoulders up off the ground. Lobo stood up, and backed off a little way. Tim saw that he was watching it all with an anxious look in his eyes, but he wasn't growling, anyway. It even seemed as if he understood, and when Shep and Danny carried Tim acoss to the line of trees, Lobo just followed.

It was a lot more comfortable lying flat on the grassy ground. "Now then," Shep said, "I'll just leave my gun with you, Danny." Tim looked up at him quickly. "Did you smell wildcat, Shep?" he asked him. "Well — " Shep said in his quiet, slow way, "tell you something, Tim. You smell 'em a lot

145

more often than you see 'em. They're around all right. That's for sure. But I wouldn't worry much about 'em this time of year." Still, Tim told himself, there was some reason why Shep had thought of leaving his gun. He guessed he'd been right about that smell, and he guessed Lobo had known about it, too. Gosh! Tim was thinking all over again, Lobo was a great dog! But would he really accept the others, though? Would he follow them down to the house, for instance? Maybe he'd have to get him on a rope, Tim thought, or something that would secure him. If I just had a belt, he thought next. He glanced over to where Lobo was standing, watching them all. He wasn't looking so anxious any more. He was just looking — watchful. And all at once Tim said in his heart, You'll just have to trust me, Lobo. You'll just have to come because you want to. As soon as he'd thought it, he knew it was the only way. He wouldn't want it any other way! I must have been crazy, he thought now, to think of putting a rope on Lobo. It would be like — like trapping him!

Shep had swung into his saddle and now he kicked up his horse and cantered off. It was a minute before Danny sat down, and in that moment Tim had time to wonder if maybe Danny was feeling

the same way he was feeling himself. Tim was
wishing that Shep could have stayed, and he was
wondering what they'd talk about, Danny and himself. With Judy, there'd be no problem. Judy would
do the talking, and then Tim would start talking,
too, without even having to think about it. With
Danny it was different. He watched Danny pull
a blade of grass and then start chewing on it. He
was looking out across the pasture, but there was
something in his eyes that seemed to be looking even
farther than that. Tim looked at Lobo again.
"Hey!" he was suddenly able to say, "you think
Lobo'll come back down to the house with us?"
Danny looked back at him briefly. "What d'you
think?" he asked, instead of answering. He'd looked
away again already. In the next minute thunder was
rumbling in the dark sky. "Storm's almost here,"
Danny said. "We'll get rain any minute. I sure hope
Dad's going to make time." Tim said, "I guess he
will. But — Dan — " he added, "about Lobo — I
mean, you figure he'll follow us down to the house?"
Danny shrugged. "Who knows?" he asked, "if you
don't?" At that he really looked at Tim. "I mean,"
he explained in a nicer tone, "I figure he's your dog.
Or else he isn't. Know what I mean?" Tim thought
about it for a minute. "I guess so," he said then.

147

"Yeah." He wasn't really sure, though. "But I mean — " he started to say, but his words were lost in a great flash of lightning that seemed to split the sky and then tear it with the noise of a great tearing sheet. "You think Shep'll be back pretty soon?" he asked anxiously. "He better!" Danny said. He had to raise his voice to make himself heard above the roar of the torrential rain that was suddenly falling like a wall of water.

Lobo came over and dropped to the ground beside Tim. Was he being protective now, or was he feeling nervous and maybe asking for protection for himself? For the first time it crossed Tim's mind that maybe Lobo needed him just as much as he needed Lobo — or more?

11

When Shep finally came back up the trail he was
closely followed by Buck riding one of the pack
horses. They'd brought a knocked-down litter, some
warm, dry clothes, and a Thermos of hot soup. "You
drenched?" Shep asked them. "Sopped," Danny
told him truthfully. "We thought you'd never get
here." Buck was rolling one of his home-made
cigarettes, but he paused to protest. "Never made
it so quick," he said. "If it wasn't for Miss Kate
bent on heatin' up some soup for you — " he licked
the cigarette paper and stuck the limp cigarette in
his mouth. Speaking around it, he finished, " — and
I don't guess you're goin' to complain about that
any." Shep was taking down the poles and the
stretch of canvas from the pack. "Smelled real
good," he said cheerfully. "Why don't you stow
away some of it while I put this litter together?"

Lobo had lifted his head when the men appeared,
and Tim kept his arm around the dog. When Buck,
bringing the Thermos, moved over toward Tim,

Lobo again gave a low, warning growl. Tim was secretly more pleased than not. It suggested the dog had really adopted him, and so he'd probably go along, all right, if only to take care of Tim. "It's all right, boy," he told him. "It's just Buck, come to help us. He's going to tote us down." Buck stopped and cocked an eyebrow at the dog. "*Us?*" he inquired. "That dog likely weighs as much as I do myself — and it appears to me he don't much like my looks." Shep laughed. "Guess Tim's got his brand on the dog," he said. "Long as you vouch for us, Tim — Here, Dan," he broke off to say, "give me a hand with these poles, will you? Seems like the canvas's shrunk. Don't guess anyone's used it for a long time." Tim had just taken a swallow of the hot soup when the memory swept into his mind of Buck and himself carrying old Mac down to the brook to be buried. He hoped Buck wasn't going to mention it. He didn't feel like thinking about it himself. He looked up anxiously at Buck. Apparently Buck got the message, but not the right one. "What's the trouble?" he asked. "Soup too hot?" Tim felt relieved. "Kind of hot," he said, "but it's good. I guess I was half starved." He remembered now that he hadn't eaten any breakfast. But he certainly didn't want to think back over all that right now, either. "Say, Buck," he said quickly, "why don't you get one of those gadgets for rolling cigarettes? I saw a feller at the rodeo using one. They came out just like real ones." Buck snorted. "*Real* ones!" he said contemptuously. "Real ones you roll yourself. Any cowpoke can't roll his own cigarettes better get off the range."

"Now then," Shep said, and he and Danny both got to their feet. The canvas was flat on the ground, neatly stretched between the two poles. When the violent, brief storm had passed over, the sun had come out again, and now the warm afternoon light slanted across the pasture and cast a glow on all their faces. Tim could see that Danny's shirt was drying out already. Buck said, "You done with that soup?" and Tim handed over the empty Thermos bottle. "All set now," Shep said. "Let's get you into a warm shirt, Tim." He shook out the roll of dry clothes and started toward Tim. Lobo got up and moved off a little. But he didn't growl this time. He knew the difference between Buck and Shep. So maybe he'd accept Aunt Kate all right, too? Tim still wasn't sure, though. "Do you suppose?" he asked anxiously, "Lobo could ride with me? I mean — if I'm holding him — " He appealed to Danny. "You're real strong," he said. "I mean — do you think you could manage — ?" Buck grunted. "Never saw anyone so loco about a dog," he said. He laughed then. "Lobo and loco," he said. "Well, *I* aim to lead down the horses." Shep glanced at him without smiling. "That's exactly what I had in mind for you, Buck," he told him. Even Danny didn't smile at Buck's joke. "I think the dog'll follow," he told Tim. "You got to start trusting him, you know." He said it firmly, but nicely, too. And now Tim thought again what he'd thought when the storm broke and Lobo moved over beside him. Maybe Lobo really needed him. It was a new idea, and he had to think some more about it. It was working in his mind, though. It came back up to the surface now, and it made him feel better.

Tim had almost forgotten how much it hurt to move, or be moved, but he was determined not to show it. He gritted his teeth and tried to concentrate on the comfort of the dry, flannel shirt. When they picked him up to get him over to the litter, it was harder, and he caught his breath in a sharp hiss. At once Lobo gave his low, warning growl again. This time they all laughed, and Danny told the dog: "You just come along now, and you can take care of Tim later." Tim gave him an appreciative smile. He was beginning to understand why Judy felt the way she did about Danny. He could be darned nice! When they lowered Tim onto the litter, Danny was as gentle as Shep. "I got this right?" Shep asked him. "Your left shoulder and your left leg's hurt?" "Left's right," Tim said.

Buck had swung back into his saddle on the pack horse, and now he reached for the reins of the other two horses. "I'll go on along down," he said, "and let Miss Kate know you're comin'." It was clear that he had no intention of following their slow progress.

Their progress was slow, all right. The ground was very uneven and Tim realized that Shep and Danny were doing their best not to joggle him. They stopped two or three times, set the littter down very carefully and took a little rest themselves. "Guess I'm more comfortable than you are," Tim said once. It was a sort of apology for all the trouble he was giving them, and it wasn't exactly true. Actually he hurt all over. But it was a dull kind of hurting by now, and he was getting a little used to it. It was a lot better than the fierce pain that stabbed him when he got an occasional jolt. For all their care, he was joggled now and again, and it startled him into groaning each time. Danny thought to speak to Lobo each time, and when they stopped, and set Tim down, the dog came up and licked Tim's face.

He was following along, all right. He wasn't going
to let Tim out of his sight. But would he follow him
into the house? That was the next question.

When they finally got down to where they could
see the ranch, Danny said, "There's a car in the
yard." Another troubling question shot through
Tim's mind. Could it be his father? He never had
found out just when it was his father might arrive.

Could he have flown out, rented a car, and got himself out to the ranch by now? The possibility gave
him such a confusion of emotions that to save his
life he couldn't have said what it was he was mostly
feeling. Anticipation? Fear? Distrust? And along
with all the rest he was feeling embarrassment.
Funny, but up to right now it hadn't occurred to
him that he'd made quite a mess of himself. Rush-

ing out of the house — taking the colt — bawling like a baby — and then getting himself really smashed up and causing all this trouble! He guessed he was a real mess, all right. And now to meet his father like this, stretched out flat and completely helpless — and then to have to hear all about his mother — His face was suddenly so hot that he knew he must have turned red. He felt as if he might start bawling again, too.

It had all gone through his mind so fast, and yet taken him so far away, that he was surprised to hear Shep saying in his quiet, slow way, "Guess the doctor's turned up," and Tim realized that it was only maybe a minute since Danny'd said, "There's a car in the yard." It made Tim feel sort of weird — and very relieved at the same time. He certainly hoped it was the doctor. His face was cooling off by now, and he felt pretty sure that it couldn't be his father yet.

The last steep pitch down to the ranch was really rough, and Tim was jolted a number of times. He knew beyond any doubt when they finally got to level ground. A minute later Shep called out, and then even Tim could see Aunt Kate holding open the kitchen door. "You're just in time," she told them. "Doctor's been here ten minutes and he's about ready to take off." Tim tried to raise his head, and gave it up. The next thing he knew Aunt Kate was looking down into his face. Her keen, searching eyes were gentler than he'd ever seen them. But when she spoke her voice was just about as crisp as ever. "Glad to see you all in one piece," she said. "Now I've got a bed fixed up in the sitting room. Bring him on in," she told Shep. "Figured, from what Buck said, he might be flat for some time," she told them. "Figured," she said next, "he might as well be handy. Those stairs to the attic are kind of steep." Tim guessed she wasn't really thinking about herself and the stairs. She was thinking about him, and what would be nicer for him. When they moved into the sitting room, he was sure of it. A bright fire was blazing on the hearth, and she'd set up a little table near the bed with covered dishes of hot food. A sweet, grateful feeling flowed over Tim. The only time he'd ever known Aunt Kate to use the sitting room was the night Judy was there. Was that last night, or the night before? He wasn't sure. But maybe Judy would come to see him, and maybe Aunt Kate had thought of that, too.

Tim was just about to ask where Lobo was when Aunt Kate said, "Never thought I'd see that dog in the house." A man who had been sitting by the fire

stood up and turned around at that moment, and
Aunt Kate said, "Here's your patient. This is Tim.
And this is Dr. Cole," she told Tim.

Shep and Danny eased Tim down onto the
opened, fresh bed. At once Lobo was beside him,
not to lick Tim's face this time, but only to rest his
chin against the bed, and look into Tim's face. The
dog was back to the rest of the room, as if it didn't
exist. He had put himself between Tim and the
others, and now Dr. Cole was saying, "Better move
the dog." Then he caught Tim's expression. "Least
until I've examined you," he added kindly. Aunt
Kate was looking at Lobo. "That's the ghost-dog, all
right," she said. "How in tarnation did you make
friends with him?" "He saved my life," Tim told
her. But Dr. Cole was waiting for him to move the
dog away from the bed. He wondered, again,
whether he could manage it. But Dan was right,
and he had to trust Lobo. He certainly had reason
enough to trust him by now. And Lobo had trusted
him! He'd trusted him enough to follow, and come
straight into the house and amongst all these strange
people. "Lie down, Lobo," Tim said. After a second's hesitation Lobo dropped to the floor, and then
crawled under the bed. Tim heard Aunt Kate say
softly, "I'll be danged." And now Dr. Cole was

leaning down and saying, "Gather you landed on your shoulder, so let's take a look at that first." A minute later he said, "Relax, Tim. I won't hurt you any more'n I got to. You get your muscles all tensed up and it's hard to know what's going on in there. O.K.?" Tim said, "O.K." but he was still thinking about Lobo and whether he could keep him or not. He was thinking about his father, too, and how it was going to be when he turned up. He thought Aunt Kate was impressed with Lobo, and that was a good sign. She might let Lobo stay. But what about his father? And how would it be when they had to go home? "I had a dog like that once," Dr. Cole was saying. "When I was about your age, as a matter of fact. It's a great breed! Guess you know what the Seeing-Eye people say: 'Only dog that's intelligent enough to know when to *disobey.*' That can be pretty important when they're taking care of the blind." He paused and smiled at Tim. "That's better," he said. "You're relaxed now." A minute later he continued, "Nearly as I can tell without an X ray, you've got a fractured clavicle. Now let's have a look at that leg."

To his surprise Tim discovered that his leg hurt more than his shoulder. Then, to his further surprise, Dr. Cole said, "Well, that's not so bad. Nothing involved but your ankle, far as I can judge." Tim had broken out in a sweat again. "Funny," he said, "but it hurts more than my shoulder now." Dr. Cole straightened and got out a cigarette. "Can't always tell by the pain," he said. "Some of the worst things don't really hurt at all, and you can get a dilly of a pain from something pretty insignificant." He blew a smoke ring, and watched it while Tim watched it, too. "Now," Dr. Cole said, turning to Aunt Kate, "I don't think there's a thing to worry about, but he better stay put till I can get him down to the Clinic for some X rays. Tomorrow — " Tim stopped listening. He was really relaxed now. In fact he'd begun to feel a little sleepy. He dropped his good arm over the edge of the bed and at once Lobo nuzzled his hand. It was a good, peaceful feeling. For the first time today — and then Aunt Kate's voice got through to him and jolted him back wide awake, and tense all over. "I'm expecting Tim's father tomorrow," she said.

Now all the jumbled feelings were starting up again. Did he want to see his father or didn't he? What was it that gave him this uneasy feeling of distrust? Why should he be afraid? Was he afraid of his father's feelings? And his own? Was it the fact that they had to talk about his mother, and what in the world could they say? His hand was still on Lobo's muzzle and now one answer leapt to his mind. His father might be coming to take him home! And would he let Tim take Lobo with him? I won't go without you, he told the dog silently. We'll run away! We'll — we'll do *something!* he promised himself fiercely.

12

Jim was eating a late breakfast the next morning when Judy stopped in to see him. Dr. Cole had made him quite comfortable with his ankle strapped and his arm trussed up and in a sling. This morning he felt mostly sore. He guessed his bruises hurt more than his breaks by now. Dr. Cole was going to pick him up later and take him to have the X rays. "Expect you got a slight concussion," he'd said when Tim told him about blacking out. "Prob'ly O.K., but we'll take a look at your head, too."

"My goodness!" Judy said the first thing. "We're going to have to teach you how to fall." She was holding a bunch of blue lupin she'd brought him, and she was wearing a blue dress. He'd never seen her in a dress before and she looked prettier than ever. But he only said, "Never mind trying to teach me to ride better?" Judy laughed. "Oh, that!" she said, which made Tim laugh, too.

Lobo was lying by the fire now, and Judy went straight over to him. He'd lifted his head and looked at her when she came in, and then just put his head down again. "Lobo!" she said softly. He raised his head again, and thumped his tail once. "He acts as if he knows you," Tim said. "He just knows," Judy said. "And isn't he beautiful? Danny told me about his coming down for help. Lobo," she told the dog, "you're just wonderful. And you saved Tim's life!" Lobo thumped his tail again. Tim was bursting with pride and pleasure, but he just said, "Hey! Those are my favorite flowers." Judy turned back to him. "Mine, too," she told him. "I guess I'd better get something to put them in," she said then, but instead she went over and sat down on the chair nearest Tim's bed.

"Tim," she said earnestly, "you prob'ly don't want to talk about it, but I feel just awful about your mother. I'm just glad you're braver than I am because I don't know what I'd do."

"I don't know what I'll do, either," Tim said. A second later he realized that here he was talking about it, after all, and for the first time, and it was — well, it was all right. "Did anyone — I mean, did anyone tell you about my father coming out?" he asked her then. Judy's face brightened. "Miss Kate told me," she said, "and I'm so glad! That's wonderful."

"Well — yeah — " he said slowly. "But, I don't

know — I feel sort of — I don't know," he said again. "It just makes me kind of — well — know what I mean?" He searched her face. Really he was asking her to tell him what he meant.

She didn't answer right away. She was really thinking about it. He could tell that. Most people would say something, fast — something nice, really, whether they meant it or not. And that was all right! But Judy was different. She was really thinking about it, and she'd say exactly what she meant. While he waited it went through his mind that he liked Judy better than just about anyone he knew.

"Do you mean — " she asked him finally, "that your father's prob'ly feeling just as bad as you do — or maybe even worse? And you don't know what to say — and maybe he won't know what to say, either? Is that what you mean?"

"I guess that's right — yeah," he agreed. He was feeling a certain qualified relief. "It sort of — mixes you all up. If he — I mean suppose he — well, Aunt Kate said something about how it's all right for a man to — you know, cry? But heck!" he finished helplessly.

Judy nodded. Her eyes were so filled with sympathy and real understanding that Tim began to feel as if he might cry again himself. Then all at once Judy's eyes changed completely. "Know what I think?" she demanded. "I think it's crazy! I mean, men and women and — and *people*, and everything. It's all right for women to cry. My mother cries whenever she wants to. So what's so darned different about men? It's crazy!" she declared again. She shook her head. "I mean, even grown people — " She suddenly leaned so far forward in her chair that Tim half expected her to pitch right over on her face. "Remember when I got all upset?" she asked him, "about Danny suddenly growing up, and all? Honestly!" she said. "The very next day he did the silliest darned thing. Honestly, you'd think he was about five years old. So *I* decided," she told him, "that maybe people don't ever *exactly* grow up. I mean — well, *altogether*," she said. "Know what I mean?"

Now she was asking him, and he no longer felt like crying. "You mean," he said, "they kind of go right on *feeling* the same way, no matter how old they get? But then maybe they figure they can't exactly *show* it any more because — well, they're *supposed* to be kind of all grown up and different, and all." Judy had started to nod and she kept right on nodding. He'd hardly ever talked to anyone who listened the way Judy was listening.

"That's right!" she said. "That's what sort of — *came* to me, I mean." Now she sat back in her chair with a thud. "Honestly, Tim," she told him, "I think you've got about the most brilliant mind I ever — well, ever talked to!" she finished. It was a minute before Tim could collect himself. Then he said, "You mean including Danny?"

"Oh!" she said, "Danny! He isn't *brilliant*. He's just — well, he's just Danny." Tim couldn't think when he'd felt so good. But after a bit he had to say, "Danny's great, though. I really like him." Judy said, "Of course. Everyone likes Danny." She stood up, "And now," she said, "I better get these flowers into some water. I'll be right back."

Tim watched her walk across the room with her pretty blue dress with the wide skirt sort of dancing around her knees. "Hey!" he called out suddenly, "How come you didn't ride over?" She turned at the door. "Dad was going to town in the truck," she told him, "so he gave me a lift. Like my dress?" she asked him unexpectedly. "It's pretty," he said. At once it struck him that he could have said a number of things more brilliant than that. But there was something about the way Judy whirled out of the room that made him think he'd done all right, after all.

Judy and Aunt Kate were talking in the kitchen. Tim could hear their voices but not their words. Their voices made a nice, soothing sound. His breakfast had been really good — bacon and scrambled eggs, and hot corn muffins. Aunt Kate had never made him corn muffins before. She always made her own butter, though, and it wasn't like any butter he'd ever eaten before. It was almost better than jam. An agreeable sleepy feeling began to steal over him. Just before closing his eyes he looked across at Lobo. He was sleeping so peacefully that Tim didn't speak to him, although he wanted to. He wondered if the doctor would let him take Lobo with him to the Clinic. He wondered when Dr. Cole might turn up. "Whenever I can find a space in the day," was all he'd said. Then Tim began to wonder when his father might get in. Maybe he'd be off at the Clinic when his father arrived, and that might be all right, too.

Lobo's legs began to twitch and move as if he were running in his dreams. A second later he woke up, and almost at once he lifted his head to look for Tim. "It's all right, boy!" Tim told him. "I'm right here." Lobo thumped his tail, and then

dropped his head back down to the floor content-
edly. Tim thought again about his new idea that
maybe he was more important to Lobo than Lobo
was to him. It gave him a slightly uncomfortable
feeling, as if he were being disloyal, and he quickly
reminded himself of Lobo's loyalty. He made up
his mind then and there that he was going to take
Lobo to town with him. Dr. Cole would simply
have to let him! Gosh! he thought, as if he were
arguing with Dr. Cole or somebody, did Lobo leave
me? He was gone only long enough to get help, and
then he came straight back again. So Tim certainly
wasn't going to leave him, especially right now before he'd got used to the house, and Aunt Kate, and
all. "You can count on that," he said aloud.

He was wide awake again by now and he hunched
himself straighter in the bed and listened for sounds
from the kitchen. Judy and Aunt Kate were still
talking. At this rate Judy might be staying for lunch.
He wasn't sure just what time it was, but he'd waked
up pretty late. A minute later Judy appeared in the
doorway carrying the lupin in a tall jug. "Dr. Cole's
coming up the road," she told him. "Miss Kate'll be
right in to help you get ready." She looked at him
anxiously. "I hope it won't hurt," she said before
setting the jug down on the mantelpiece.

"Hey!" he said, "where you going?" At the door she turned to say, "I expect Dad'll be along any minute. If he's late, Miss Kate's going to give me lunch. I hope you're going to be all right," she said again just before disappearing.

Tim heard Aunt Kate's swinging step coming down the hall, and then the telehone rang. Probably Shep, Tim thought comfortably, saying he was going to be late. In the next instant he had tensed all over. Aunt Kate had said, "Matthew? Where are you?" She was talking to Tim's father. I'll round up Buck, or Trip, and send 'em in to fetch you," she said next. "If you don't mind waiting around — take about — what's that?" Tim felt as if he was holding his breath. Or maybe his breath was holding him. He tried to breathe naturally and it wasn't easy. He had a wild, trapped feeling and it seemed to be mainly located in his chest. "Why don't you take the bus, then?" Aunt Kate was saying now. "This time of year there's three a day, anyway. More on weekends. Let's see — today's — what's that?" she asked again. "That's expensive," she said. His father must have said that he'd rent a car. He was at the airport, of course, and that was — anyway fifty miles down the canyon. "Well, it's up to you," Aunt Kate said next. "Your place, I'd take the bus, or wait for one of the boys. You're free to use the truck here, you know." The silence was longer this time. "All right," she said finally. And then, "He's O.K.," she said, saying it fast so Tim knew his father had asked about him and Aunt Kate wasn't going into it all over the phone. "Be glad to see you," she added, like an afterthought. Tim heard the receiver drop back into place.

"All set?" It was Dr. Cole's voice sounding from the kitchen door. Everything was happening all at once, and now Tim had a different sort of wild feeling. He felt like — well, he felt kind of like a checker that was being pushed helplessly this way and that way across the checkerboard.

13

When Dr. Cole drove into the yard bringing Tim and Lobo back from the Clinic, Tim's father and Aunt Kate were sitting in the sun on the kitchen steps. His father got up at once and came over to Tim's side of the car. It was reassuring, after all, to see him. He looked so natural, and he was even smiling. "Hi, Tim!" he said. "Shall I help you out?" He wasn't looking worried, and he certainly didn't look as if he was apt to cry, ever. "Did kind of a job on yourself, didn't you?" he said, but he wasn't sounding critical. He didn't seem to feel as if Tim had made a real mess of himself, first to last, and now Tim realized how worried he'd been about that, too. "I guess I did," Tim admitted. "But I can get along all right. As long as I don't really put my weight down on my foot, Dr. Cole says I can get around." His father looked into the back of the car. "So this is the famous dog," he said. "Hello, feller!" He opened the car door. "Hear you saved Tim's life." His voice was just right. He certainly knew how to talk to a dog, and Tim felt grateful. "Thank you, Lobo," his father was saying. He talked to the dog as if he were another person, and a person he respected. "He's a nice shepherd, Tim," he said now. "Looks like the dog you've always wanted, doesn't he?"

Tim had edged himself out of the car, and holding onto the door, was standing there on his good foot. "He is!" he told his father. "So I can take him home with me, can't I?" he asked quickly. "I mean — I've got to!" he added. Lobo had got out of the car when Tim did, and now Tim's father closed the back door. "We'll have to talk about that, Tim," he said. Tim's heart sank. When his father said, "We'll see," or "We'll have to talk about that," it generally meant just one thing. He was going to say "No." He always said it nicely, and he always sort of consulted Tim. He tried to appeal to Tim's reason, and to make him feel as if the decision was really Tim's. Tim used to fall for it, too. But now he knew better, and this time he wasn't going to fall for it! His jaws were clamped so tight that his face began to hurt. Then I won't go home, he was telling himself. I'll stay here! We'll run away, he thought again. They might go back up to the high pasture, he and Lobo. They might find Lobo's cave. He must have had some cave, Tim figured, where he'd spent the winters and where he'd maybe spent the nights. He must have had some hideout where he could sleep in safety, out of reach of marauding wild animals. They could stay there, Tim thought, until his father went back, anyway. We'll do something! he said to himself fiercely again.

Dr. Cole and Tim's father had introduced themselves, and now they all moved toward the house, Dr. Cole helping Tim a little. "Wonderful air out here," Tim's father was saying. "I'd almost forgotten what it's like." Dr. Cole chuckled. "Just don't forget how the altitude catches up on you," he suggested. "Air makes you feel like you could move a mountain single-handed. The next thing you know, you fold like a pricked balloon. Till you get used to it." Tim's father said, "I could use some sleep." For a swift, uneasy moment Tim thought of his mother. Well, he thought of them both, his mother and his father, going through it all together — while he was left clean out of it.

They'd got to the kitchen door by now and Aunt Kate, who was holding it open for them, said, "Sleep for a week, if you want to. Couldn't have come to a better place for it." Dr. Cole agreed, "That's for sure. Probably won't want to do anything else, for a bit." "Meantime," Aunt Kate said, leading them in to the sitting room, "I'm going to feed you both. You just sit down and I'll bring in a tray," she told them, while Tim sat down on the edge of his bed, and Lobo went over to the fire. "I'll just go out to the car with Dr. Cole," Tim's father said, "and get the run-down on your injuries, Tim." So for a few minutes Tim was alone with Lobo. After a bit he said, "Dad's all right, isn't he, boy?" He wanted intensely for them to like each other, Lobo and his father. And they seemed to have got off to a good start. Lobo hadn't growled once. Well, his father really understood dogs. And Lobo — Tim smiled to himself remembering Judy saying, "He just knows." But a minute later Tim was scowling. He could practically hear his father saying, "I love dogs! And that's the very reason I won't have a big dog in the city. It isn't fair to the dog. And this fellow who's had the run of the mountains — " Oh, Tim could just hear it all, a fair, sensible argument that he'd never be able to talk down. And suppose his father wanted to take Tim home right away — or in a few days from now? It was all very well, Tim realized at this moment, to think about running away and hiding out. He couldn't run anywhere as long as he was in this shape. He could just about hobble around. He wondered how long his father might be planning to stay. And he wondered how long it might be before he himself was mended.

Instead of Aunt Kate coming in with their lunch, Tim's father came back carrying the big tray. "Nice fellow, Cole," he said. "Seems to know his business, too. Now — you as hungry as I am?" he asked cheerfully. "Had a cup of coffee with Aunt Kate," he said, "but I thought I'd wait to eat with you." He was uncovering the dishes, and now he pulled up a second little table for himself.

When he'd settled himself on the nearest chair and they'd begun to eat, he said, "You look good, Tim." His eyes twinkled briefly. "Apart from being a bit banged up, that is," he added. "You look as if the summer's done you a lot of good, the way I thought it would." He smiled. "Guess I don't have to ask you how you like it here," he said. "It's great!" Tim said. "I wish we lived here." It was his chance to make his pitch, and he grabbed it. "Do I have to go home?" he asked, and now he'd lost all interest in what he was eating. "I mean — " His father said, "I think I know what you mean." He was looking so serious now that Tim told himself he was in for it. Everything he'd been worrying about was going to come up right now. He was sure of it. His mother

175

— but then his father was talking again. "Tim," he said, "I wanted to tell you myself. I guess Aunt Kate told you that." Tim nodded. His father had stopped eating now, too. Tim had not only stopped eating, he began to wish he'd never started. It seemed to be all churning around inside him. "The way things were, Tim," his father went on, "it was better. That's a hard thing to say, and God knows — " his voice faltered and for an awful minute Tim thought he was going to break down. "Did — I mean — did Mother think it was better?" he asked, saying it very fast into the frightening pause. "Did she *know?*" he said, "I mean." Now his father nodded. When he was able to speak again he said simply, "Yes, she knew. That's really why we thought you should — " Tim broke in. "You mean you knew in the first place?" he said, and even to himself he sounded angry and sort of accusing. It wasn't any way he'd ever spoken to his father before. But this wasn't a way he'd ever felt before. "You mean you *knew*," he went on, "and you didn't tell me. And you sent me — " Now his father interrupted him, and now he sounded almost angry, too. "Yes, we knew, Tim, and we had to make that decision. It wasn't easy, I can tell you! It was about the hardest thing we ever had to do. We went over

it and over it," he said. "We thought about *every-thing*. But most of all we tried to think about you." Tim looked away from his father's face. It made him feel — sort of ashamed, as if his father were lying to him, and expecting him to believe the lie. "Tim!" his father said. He said it with such force that it was as if he could make Tim look at him, and listen to him, and even believe him with the power of his voice alone. "Your mother was very brave. I never knew anyone braver. And — you listen to me, Tim — I guess there was only one thing she couldn't have been brave about, and that would be having anything bad happen to you. You hear me, Tim? She loved you very much!"

Tim half knew that it was a crazy thing to think, and so he just managed not to say it. He just managed not to say, "Then why did she leave me?" That was the worst thing that could happen to him, and if she cared so much — Now his father was talking again and it was almost as if he'd read Tim's mind. "She'd have done *anything* not to leave you," he said, "if she could have. But she didn't have anything to say about it. Nobody does, you know." After a second he said, "Tim!" again. "You're old enough to know that." Tim suddenly remembered Aunt Kate saying, "You think you can stop death?"

After a minute he was able to look at his father again. "But then — " he said, "why couldn't I have stayed? I mean — " His father said, "You mean, then why weren't you old enough to be included?" Tim guessed it was exactly what he meant.

For the first time it was his father who looked away. He rubbed a hand across his eyes. "You've got a lot of feeling about that, haven't you?" he said. But it was if he was telling himself, more than he was really asking Tim. "Maybe we were wrong," he said then. "But we went over it and over it," he repeated, in a tired-sounding voice this time, "we did the best we could. It *seemed* — " and now he met Tim's eyes again. "You know how close you always were to your mother. So it seemed as if you needed some — well, space. The way we figured it," he said, and now for the first time Tim believed that he wasn't lying, but was telling Tim exactly the way it was, exactly what they'd thought and decided. "The way we figured it," his father said again, "you needed to get some self-reliance. You needed to do some growing up, and get so you could — well, stand on your own feet a bit. If you had to get along without her, then we figured you had to — sort of get a little head start. Get a little used to being on your own. You following me,

179

Tim?" he stopped to ask. There was nothing Tim could say but, "Yes." It was true, too. His father always could explain things, and now he was explaining this. Tim didn't feel much better, right away. But at least he didn't think, any longer, that his father was trying to pull the wool over his eyes. "I think — " his father was saying slowly, "it was the hardest thing your mother ever had to do — to make that decision, I mean. It was like — it was like giving you up already, before she actually had to. Can you understand that, Tim? She could only bring herself to do it *for you* — because she figured it was the best thing for you. You've got to *know* that, Tim, because it's God's truth!"

Tim picked up the plate from his knees and set it back on the end table. "What are we — " he had to swallow before he could go on. "What are we going to do now?" he asked. A faint, brief smile flickered in his father's eyes. "Good for you, Tim," he said then. "I'm proud of you." Tim remembered his mother saying so many times, "I'm proud of you, Tim." This was the first time he could remember his father saying it.

His father had pushed away his plate, too, and now he got out a cigarette and lighted it. "I've been thinking about that, Tim," he said. "Do you remember saying, a bit back, that you'd like to live here? And you said, 'Do I have to go home?' That got to me!" he said. "I mean — what's home? I don't know if you were thinking about that — but I was!" he said with vigor. He sat back, and now a real smile was spreading over his face. "We had a really nice home, Tim," he said. "We'll never forget that. Except — " he added, with a changed expression, "you never had the dog you wanted. I'm sorry about that. I really am! I kept thinking — next year. We'll move out into the country — well, that's the kind of thing you don't know about — you *can't* know about, I guess — until you get caught up in all the pressures yourself." He looked down. "Now I figure," he said, "I could have done it sooner." He straightened. "But now," he went on, "why not? Whether we like it or not, we've got to start all over again. So what's the matter with starting here?"

Tim began to feel as if something was popping inside him, like a balloon that was getting ready to burst. "You mean — " he said. "No kidding?" he asked. "Gosh!" he said. All sorts of pleasant pictures were flashing through his mind. Aunt Kate — and Lobo. Shep and Judy and Dan. All the new friends he'd made. All the new life that was opening around him. "But what about your practice, though?" he suddenly asked his father.

"Been thinking about that," his father told him. "Thought about it all the way out on the plane, as a matter of fact. I took on a young assistant this summer," he said. "Had to!" He glanced at Tim. "I was spending most of my time in the hospital with your mother. So I figure — he can take it over." He sort of smiled, briefly. "Nice practice — all ready made. I really built that up," he said. He shrugged. And then, abruptly, he squared his shoulders and sat up straight. "For us, it means really starting again," he said. "I mean, from scratch. But what have we got to lose? Had a talk with Aunt Kate before you got back. She's fighting mad about the so-called vet in this area." He chuckled. "Matter of fact," he said, "she's been after me from way back. Never could understand why I wanted to settle in the city and take care of what she calls those 'pampered pets.' Out here they have cattle, and horses, and real working dogs — and a no-good vet to take care of them, from what she tells me. And I guess," he said, "no one's in a better position to know." He looked straight at Tim again. "It would really cut down our income for awhile," he said. "So — what d'you say?"

Tim couldn't say anything just at first. He felt like

laughing, or bursting out crying, and he really didn't know which. He made a real effort, though, and came out with: "No kidding?"

"No kidding, Tim," his father said so earnestly that there was no doubt left in Tim's mind. "You mean — we can live here with Aunt Kate, and all?" he asked. "Well — " his father said, "we've got to work that all out. Aunt Kate says 'Yes.' Wants us, as a matter of fact. Claims she needs us, even. She's getting on — " He paused, and then, speaking more quickly, "Says she's got no one to leave the place to. Never mind about that," he said. "Give us a little time and we'll be paying our own way. Here's the way I figure it — we'll put up a house of our own. Aunt Kate's determined to give us a chunk of land right now. Meantime, until we get settled, we can stay here and let her get away for a bit. She'd like to do a little traveling, you know — see some more of the world before she dies. So, we can take care of the ranch for her — "

Tim had stopped really listening. There was one more unresolved question troubling his mind, and when his father said, "she's getting on" it floated right up to the surface. His father must have read it in his face because now he was saying, "I think I know what's on your mind, Tim. You want to know how come your mother couldn't live as long as Aunt Kate." He leaned forward in his chair and scrubbed out his cigarette in the ashtray, and said, "The thing is, Tim, people die at different ages. Sometimes babies die. Real babies!" He lit another cigarette. "Take a war," he said, "and the young fellows die and the old folks go right on living. Thing is," he continued, "everyone's got to do it. Sooner or later," he said, "everyone who's born has got to die. You can't escape it." He sat back. "Guess all I can say," he told Tim a minute later, "is what I've been saying to myself, over and over — in anything and everything, it isn't the *quantity* that counts, it's the *quality*. The quality of your mother was something beautiful — and if she'd lived to be a hundred years old it couldn't have been any greater." He sighed a deep sigh. "We have to remember that, Tim," he said. "We have to remember her. We have to talk about her as time goes by and remember all the fine, lovely things she was."

Now it swept back into Tim's mind how Aunt Kate had stood there, down by the brook, and talked about old Mac and how he had used to be as a puppy, splashing in the water and trying to catch himself a trout. When Tim had waked up the next morning he had thought about it all, and he had decided that it was good. He remembered, too, how Judy had helped him to talk a little about his mother, and how it had made him feel better.

Thinking about Judy, he glanced at the jug of lupin that she'd left on the mantelpiece. "Remember?" he was suddenly able to say, "how Mother always looked when she found a new wildflower?" He even had to laugh a little. "I used to feel sometimes," he confessed, "as if she really liked flowers better than she liked me." His father laughed a little, too. "She liked everything beautiful," he said. For a minute Tim was afraid that his father was going to cry, after all. He watched him dash his hand at his eyes, and it made him look away. But when he looked back again his father was almost smiling. "Your mother never liked anything in this world better than she liked you, Tim," he said.

The beginning of a peaceful sort of feeling was creeping over Tim. "Hey, Dad," he said, "isn't Lobo great?" His father, too, looked across to where Lobo was sleeping by the fire. "He's as fine a dog as I've ever encountered," he answered. "And that takes in a pretty big group."

As though he had heard them, or somehow sensed

their interest, Lobo stirred and shifted his position. Then he lifted his head, looked at them both, and thumped his tail on the floor. Tim's father really smiled now. "Aunt Kate told me about him," he said. "The ghost-dog. But why don't you tell me, Tim, about how you found him, and made friends with him, and everything?"

It was nice of his father, and Tim appreciated it. But right now there was something more important that he needed to say. He wouldn't have believed, even an hour ago, that he could say it. But now he could.

"I have to tell you, Dad," he said, "that I figured I'd run away, or something, if you wouldn't let me keep Lobo. But now — well, if we had to, I guess I'd go back with you. I mean, I would!" he said fiercely. "Even if I had to leave Lobo with Aunt Kate." He managed to almost smile. "I guess, anyway," he said, "I couldn't ever give her anything better!" At that he had to stop because even now the thought of giving up Lobo made his throat get tight.

"Thank you, Tim," his father said so seriously that Tim knew he really understood. "You couldn't give *me* anything better than that," he said. He was

187

looking at Tim in a way that he'd never exactly looked at him before. It came to Tim that his father was looking at him the way he'd look at another grown person. It came to him next that his father wasn't just understanding him — they were understanding each other.

About the Author:

Ruth Peabody Harnden was born and grew up in Boston. She attended Radcliffe College and Trinity College, Dublin, Ireland. Miss Harnden has written two novels and several short stories for adults. *The High Pasture* is her second book for younger readers. The first was *Golly and the Gulls*.